Reinaldo Arenas was born near Holguín, Cuba, in 1943. His second novel, later known as *Hallucinations,* had to be smuggled out of his country to be published. When it appeared in France, it brought him international fame and a nomination for the Prix Médicis. He wrote nine novels, three books of stories, two volumes of poetry, plays, essays and a memoir—much of it in the last ten years of his life in New York. Suffering from AIDS, he committed suicide in 1990.

Dolores M. Koch was born in Cuba and holds a Ph.D. in Latin American literature. At Arenas's request, she translated his novel *The Doorman* and afterward, his memoir, *Before Night Falls,* which was a *New York Times* Best Book of the Year. She lives in New York City.

Also by Reinaldo Arenas

Mona and Other Tales

REINALDO ARENAS

Selected and Translated by

Dolores M. Koch

VINTAGE BOOKS
A Division of Random House, Inc.
New York

A VINTAGE ORIGINAL, SEPTEMBER 2001

FIRST EDITION

Some of the stories in this collection were first published in English in the following:
"The Glass Tower" in *Grand Street 61* (New York, 1997). "Halley's Comet" in *Hopscotch: A Cultural Review* (Vol. 2, No. 1, Duke University Press, 2000). "Mona" in
The Penguin Book of International Gay Writing, edited by Mark Mitchell (New York:
Viking, 1995). "Something Is Happening on the Top Floor" in *Dream with No
Name: Contemporary Fiction from Cuba*, edited by Juana Ponce de Leon and Esteban
Rios Rivera (New York: Seven Stories Press, 1999). "Traitor" in *Index on Censorship:
Lost Words*, edited by Alberto Manguel and Craig Stephenson (London: Orion, 1996).

All of the stories in this collection were originally published in the following Spanish
language works: *Adiós a mamá (De La Habana a Nueva York)*, copyright © 1995 by
the Estate of Reinaldo Arenas, copyright © 1995 by Ediciones Altera, S. L. (Barcelona:
Ediciones Altera). *Viaje a La Habana (Novela en Tres Viajes)*, copyright © 1990 by
Reinaldo Arenas (Miami: Ediciones Universal). *Termina el desfile*, copyright © 1981
by Reinaldo Arenas, copyright © 1981 by Editorial Seix Barral, S. A. (Barcelona: Seix
Barral). *Final de un cuento*, copyright © 1991 by Reinaldo Arenas (Huelva, Spain:
Diputacion Provincial de Huelva). "The Empty Shoes," originally published as
"Los zapatos vacios," copyright © 1999 by the Estate of Reinaldo Arenas (*Encuentro*,
No. 12/13, Spring/Summer 1999, Madrid).

Library of Congress Cataloging-in-Publication Data
Arenas, Reinaldo, 1943–
Mona and other tales / Reinaldo Arenas ; translated by Dolores M. Koch— 1st ed.
p. cm.
ISBN 0-375-72730-2
1. Arenas, Reinaldo, 1943—Translations into English. I. Koch, Dolores. II. Title.
PQ7390.A72 A24 2001
863'.64—dc21   2001026552

Book design by Christopher M. Zucker

www.vintagebooks.com

Printed in the United States of America
10   9   8   7   6   5   4   3   2   1

Contents

Acknowledgments

My thanks to Margarita and Jorge Camacho, Juan Abreu, Dr. Olivier Ameisen, Thomas Colchie, and the many other people who made Arenas's life and work possible. And thanks to Lee Paradise for his support and valuable suggestions, which helped make this translation possible.

Reinaldo had a tremendous ability to create very loyal friends as well as enemies. To all of them, this translation is dedicated.

The Joyful Sixties in Latin American Literature

I HAD TO PREPARE a paper to be read at a university conference. It was going to be about one of the most important moments in Spanish American literature: the novels of the sixties. I was writing it on the train while on my way there. The train crossed faceless town after faceless town in the United States, no doubt through one of the most boring landscapes on earth. That landscape should have incited me to write, since there was nothing to distract me from delving into my paper on the joyful sixties. "The Joyful Sixties," that would be the title of my presentation. And the topic, the reasons that during an eight-year period, from 1962 to 1970, Latin America produced more than ten extraordinary novels. This has always amazed me, knowing that it would perhaps take centuries for an event so unique to be repeated.

Let me try to enumerate quickly, at the speed of the train, these already classic works. In 1962, *Explosion in a Cathedral (El siglo de las luces),* by Alejo Carpentier, appears in Mexico and in France. It is an imposing linguistic structure, orchestrated like a piece of music, which offers an epic vision of the failure of the French Revolution, under the guise of which lurks, sometimes overtly and sometimes allegorically, the failure of the Cuban revolution. This is, without any doubt, Carpentier's masterpiece. It is published first in French, and then in Spanish in Mexico, before appearing in Cuba in 1963. In that same year Julio Cortázar publishes *Hopscotch (Rayuela),* and Mario Vargas Llosa, *The Time of the Hero (La ciudad y los perros).* The former is the novel *par excellence* of alienation and cross-acculturation, the novel of the big city and of the intellectual who feels lost in it and tries to find his Latin American identity in Paris, in the midst of an absurd and quite often unwelcoming world; we watch the daily adventures of a new Ulysses who will never make it to Ithaca. And *The Time of the Hero* introduces a young writer who at twenty-five wrote a masterpiece about violence, machismo, and Latin American militarism, using quite an innovative technique and a kind of language that seemed to break new ground with its fists.

In 1966 a monumental work, *Paradiso,* by José Lezama Lima, appears in Havana. Open to infinite interpretations, it is not a novel but a compendium of all novels (and of antinovels as well). Its text ranges from the sacred to the erotic. Moreover, *Paradiso* is the most portentous verbal monument in the literature of Latin America. Its publication caused a commotion that perplexed most of its readers and angered the Cuban government bureaucracy to the extent that no more editions were published in Cuba, even though it was out of print in just one week.

In the following year, 1967, Latin American literature is again enriched by at least a couple of one-of-a-kind works: *Three Trapped Tigers (Tres tristes tigres),* by Guillermo Cabrera Infante, and *One Hundred Years of Solitude (Cien años de soledad),* by Gabriel García Márquez.* *Three Trapped Tigers* plays not only with the possibilities of the Spanish language, and of Cuban expressions and Havana's street voices, particularly of its nightlife then, but also with witticisms and puns, and even new words of the author's invention: language as a tool at the writer's disposal, not as sacred dogma. *One Hundred Years of Solitude* is the work of a genius of the divertissement, following the tradition of authors such as Jorge Luis Borges, Alejo Carpentier, Juan Rulfo, and, of course, William Faulkner, and fusing them in a burst of inventiveness that he illuminated with incessant fireworks. A great roundabout, ingenious joyride through that world that is Latin America, always about to collapse, all stupor and chaos . . . But the total collapse, and even the nostalgia of that collapse, climaxes in *The Obscene Bird of Night (El obsceno pájaro de la noche),* by José Donoso, a novel published in 1970. With this perfect work on the crumbling of a family that symbolizes the whole human race, the cycle of masterpieces published within an eight-year period came to an end.

*Arenas does not mention the international literary stir created when he was not yet twenty-five years old by his second novel, *El mundo alucinante* (translated into English twice—first as *Hallucinations,* then as *The Ill-Fated Peregrinations of Fray Servando*). It had won a prize in a national competition, but was refused publication for political reasons. After being smug-

The fact that during the sixties Latin America produced at least eight (my enumeration has been minimal) extraordinary novels that transformed and enriched not only Spanish American literature, but that of the Western world, up to then deep into the lethargic nouveau roman, continues to be for me a source of wonder, and I feel I can only offer a tentative interpretation. . . . While I was writing these notes and trying to find a reasonable explanation for this synchronized eclosion of lasting works, my train continued moving through the same essentially boring landscape: identical trees, one after the other, the same gas stations, another (or the same?) Burger King, the same prescribed nothingness, the same programmed boredom for hundreds and hundreds of miles. . . . Unquestionably, it was better to delve into the joyful sixties and to attempt to determine what triggered such literary splendor.

The joyful sixties! That might be precisely the key to the conditions that enabled Latin American writers (with three Cuban authors among them) to produce novels of true distinction. Joy is a state of grace, a time of hope, faith, enthusiasm, abandon, desire, playfulness, invention, rebellion, incessant exploration. Joy, great joy, is an illusive state, a collective euphoria. These were the joyful sixties because the world had been shaken by a sexual revolution and, one way or another, prejudices had been swept away. The joyful sixties because young men were then proud of their beautiful and rebellious long hair, and young women did not blush anymore at the idea, and practice, of free love. The joyful sixties because a

---

gled out of Havana, the novel was first published in France in 1968, receiving a Prix Médicis nomination for best foreign novel. Arenas details these events in his memoir, *Before Night Falls,* also an international success, which became an American film of the same title, in 2000. —DMK

musical revolution had also taken over the world, and the Beatles with their unique songs had broken all barriers of common incommunication. All curtains drew open—whether political ones or those of prudishness or bad taste—and made way for poetry; nothing could stop the avalanche of joyousness and vitality.

These were the joyful sixties because while youth proclaimed that the center of power was the ability to imagine, hippies were decorating the cars of bureaucrats with flowers. The joyful sixties because we found more exultation in a canto than in a hymn, and because new hymns were invented, and because after so many years of repression, of self-inhibition and hypocrisy, true freedom had been discovered. The joyful sixties because then film masterpieces flooded the movie screens, instead of the commercial inanities now overflowing everywhere. The joyful sixties because young people, even in Cuba, would brazenly jump into the ocean wearing their best clothes, or the sounds of a guitar strumming would burst forth in an evening full of promises. The joyful sixties because the distant scents of spring in Prague would reach us at La Rampa in Havana . . . No, it wasn't only that Latin America was going through a most powerful romantic movement, or that Cuba had been recognized as the cradle of literary modernism, or that during the thirties some outstanding books had been written. The fact was that a new creative vitality, sustained no doubt by those traditions, needed to forge ahead because the conditions were auspicious and the public somehow demanded it. The moment of liberation had finally come, the beginning of a new age, and we were eager for adventure, feeling at least in possession of our outsized dreams, or of the late-night air, while we were still able to enjoy it. Another kind of revolution had also started in Cuba, and it had toppled years of tyranny.

It was natural then, in such an environment saturated by the energy in the air crossing over all boundaries, that a series of unique works would spring forth. The moment called for boldness, and therefore for creativity (and here again, another gas station, another Burger King, the uniform darkness of another stand of pine trees, of the flat and infinite horizon where the train moved along as through an interminable tunnel). This vitality, which had been gestating for a very long time but exploded in the sixties, also impregnated the creative talents of many writers. And it must be recognized that many of these writers had then made exclusive commitments to freedom and creativity. Even Alejo Carpentier was a quasi-dissident, writing in Paris or in La Guadalupe, and getting his works published in Mexico before Cuba. Cabrera Infante was already installed in what would later be his notorious London basement flat. And his neighbor was Vargas Llosa. Cortázar roamed Paris, not yet an unconditional militant of a dogmatic ideology. Lezama Lima subverted with his laughter and audacity his old house at Trocadero 162, and in an act of provocation, made an appearance at the revolutionary UNEAC [Cuban Writers and Artists Union] with an enormous Christian silver cross dangling from his front pants pocket. Lezama looked like an oversize hippie with an enormous medallion. Even García Márquez was then an elusive journalist who escaped from Prensa Latina, a news agency, and was writing feverishly in his modest Mexico City apartment.

The Latin American novel of the sixties, one of the most important events of this century, was not the product of a movement, nor of a group of writers working out of their comfortable offices (as it was for the new French novel), but was rather the product of a group of adventurers and pariahs who had made the whole world into their own homeland, and creativity into their only faith. Even Lezama Lima, a recluse in Old Havana, was more cosmopolitan than Marco Polo.

After this apologia or disquisition, call it what you will, I needed only to sink myself into those joyful sixties, and go back to the times when we still felt alive because we had dreams, and great literature could be written because we had not yet lost our innocence. . . . But now, suddenly, the train is passing by a sports arena. In the twilight I see a few young men, athletic and carefree, jumping and throwing a ball into the basket. And this image inevitably blasts me into the present. And I see myself just as I am, a product of the sixties, already in the shadow of the somber nineties. Someone who cannot identify, belong, blend in with those carefree youths throwing the ball into the air, no matter how much he wants to (and I do want to). Those young men can be totally involved in their activity because they do not carry around in their souls the obsession of a truncated dream, of a past that promised a vital future and ended up in a revolutionary concentration camp. In our lifetimes, neither I nor any Cubans of my generation in exile now, those of us who came from the future, those of us who have suffered and still suffer an unbroken chain of infamies or misfortunes, none of us shall ever again be able to throw a ball in the air with such carefree abandon, no matter how much we want to, no matter how desperately we try.

A weight that cannot be lifted hangs over each of our gestures, over each of our words, for having gone through an experience that cannot be properly expressed: the frustration of having been witnesses and actors during the glorious sixties, of having dreamed of a revolution that in every sense turned into a killing field, of having dreamed of a future that, instead of bringing us forward, had a regressive nature that devoured us and then spit us out (those of us who were not completely crushed) on this intolerable and feverish sandpit, or on the frozen plains whipped by all sorts of winds, including that of our own discontent.

The others, those who did not come from Cuba, those who have not gone through this experience, could perhaps live in the United States in a kind of limbo at least, where the curse of memory and of disappointment would not keep battering them. But for us, who possess the overwhelming lucidity of having come out of an inferno, no illusions are possible. We have suffered and endured successive degradations. The degradation of absolute poverty during the so-called period of the republic and under Fulgencio Batista's tyranny; the degradation of power under Castro's dictatorship; and the degradation brought by the need for American dollars under the current system. We lead double and even triple lives at the same time, whether we want to or not, which actually means we do not really live in any of them.

Our condition as ghosts is perfect and permanent. An enormous circus tent has fallen over our ideals. An angry frustration is our source of energy and pushes us forward. We live on fury, indignation, rage, alienation, and the desperation of trying to hold on to a world that exists only in our hopes. We are nourished by the memory of an ocean at sunset, of a unique book that understood us, read in a park under a tree, of the scent exuded by our houseplants when we came into a home that no longer exists, of a street that we shall never cross again, and a starry sky that vanishes up above, and we with it.

Somehow, out of all of this, someone might be able to create good literature in the United States, in Spanish. After all, our tradition is that of a bereft child. . . . But the one thing of which I am completely certain is that we shall never again be able to throw a ball in the air with the same ease, with that joyful abandon, with the innocence of those young men I saw briefly while my train continued its implacable rush toward the place where I had to read my presentation.

Miami, 1988

Delivered at the award ceremony for the Letras de Oro literary prizes

Mona and Other Tales

The Empty Shoes

GOSH! WHEN DID THIS HAPPEN? Heaven knows. . . . A while back, no date I can remember—everything was always so much the same that it was really difficult to distinguish one month from the next. Oh, but January was different. You know, January is the month of the *upitos* and the bellflowers, but it is also the month when the Three Wise Men pay us a visit.

The grass by the window was tall enough for their horses, and my shoes, a little bashful because they had holes in their tips, were there, waiting, openmouthed and a bit damp with evening dew.

It will soon be midnight.

"They will come after you're asleep," my cousin had whispered in a confidential tone. "And they will leave your gifts on top of the shoes." When I am asleep! But I couldn't fall asleep, I was hearing the crickets chirping outside, and I thought I heard steps too; but no, it was not them.

To sleep. I had to fall asleep, but how? My shoes were there on the windowsill, waiting.

I have to think about something else so I can fall asleep. Yes, that's it, I'll think about something else: "Tomorrow we have to trim the flight feathers and fill the water tank. After that I'll go by the brook and bring back a basket of honey berries. . . . I should not have brought down that nest that had two naked baby birds with gaping beaks and a look of fear in their eyes. . . ."

I woke up. It was so early that only a few scant rays of light were coming through the window. Almost blindly I walked to the window. How many surprises, I thought, were awaiting me. . . . But no. I touched the moist leather of my shoes: they were empty, completely empty.

Then my mother came and kissed me in silence, caressed my wet eyes with hands tired of washing dishes, nudged me softly to the edge of the bed, and slipped the shoes on my feet. "Come," she whispered then, "the coffee is ready." Then I went out and got soaked with dew. I had some flight feathers to trim.

Everything was so beautiful outside. So many bellflowers. So many of them you could walk over them without stepping on the earth, and so many *upito* flowers covering the ground that you couldn't see the holes in my shoes anymore.

Havana, 1963

The Glass Tower

EVER SINCE HE HAD ARRIVED in Miami, after the veritable odyssey of escaping his native country, noted Cuban author Alfredo Fuentes had not written a single line.

For some reason, since the day he arrived—and it had already been five years—he had found himself accepting all kinds of invitations to speak at conferences, to participate in cultural events or intellectual gatherings, and to attend literary cocktail and dinner parties where he was inevitably the guest of honor and, therefore, never given any time to eat, much less to think about his novel—or perhaps story—the one he had been carrying around in his head for years, and whose characters, Berta, Nicolás, Delfín, Daniel, and Olga, constantly vied for his attention, urging him to deal with their respective predicaments.

Berta's moral integrity, Nicolás's firm stance against mediocrity, Delfín's keen intelligence, Daniel's solitary spirit, and Olga's sweet and quiet wisdom not only clamored for the attention that he was unable to offer, they also reproached him constantly, Alfredo felt, because of the time he was spending with other people.

Most regrettable of all was that Alfredo hated those gatherings, but was incapable of refusing a gracious invitation (and what invitation isn't gracious?). He always accepted. Once there, he would be so brilliant and charming that he had earned a reputation, particularly among local writers, as a frivolous man who was something of a show-off.

On the other hand, if he were to turn down invitations to such gatherings at this point, everyone (including those who were critical of his facile eloquence) would consider it evidence of inferior breeding, selfishness, even a false sense of superiority. Thus, Alfredo found himself caught in an intricate web: he was well aware that if he continued to accept the endless flow of invitations, he would never write another word, and if he didn't, his prestige as a writer would soon fade into oblivion.

But it was also true that Alfredo Fuentes, rather than being at the center of those obliging crowds, would have much preferred to be alone in his small apartment—that is, alone with Olga, Delfín, Berta, Nicolás, and Daniel.

So pressing were his characters' appeals and so eager was he to respond that just a few hours earlier he had vowed to suspend all social activities and devote himself entirely to his novel—or story, since he didn't yet know exactly where all this might lead him.

Yes, tomorrow he was definitely going to resume his solitary and mysterious occupation. Tomorrow, because tonight it would be practically impossible for him not to attend the large party being given in his honor by the grande dame of the Cuban literary circles in Miami, Señora Gladys Pérez Campo, whom H. Puntilla had nicknamed "the Haydée Santamaría of the exile community."*

This event, however, was not merely cultural, but also had a practical purpose. Gladys had promised the writer that she would lay the foundation, that very evening, for a publishing house that would print the manuscripts that he had, at great risk, smuggled out of Cuba. Alfredo, incidentally, didn't have a penny to his name and this, of course, could give him a tremendous financial boost, as well as help to promote the works of other important but still unknown writers less fortunate than Alfredo, who already had five books to his credit.

"The publishing project will be a success," Gladys had assured him on the phone. "The most prominent people in Miami will support you. They will all be here tonight. I am expecting you at nine, without fail."

At five to nine, Alfredo crossed the vast, manicured garden toward the main door of the Pérez Campo mansion. The scent of flowers swept over him in waves, and he could hear pleasant melodies emanating from the top floor of the residence. As he listened to the music, Alfredo placed his hand

---

Haydée Santamaría was the director of the government publishing house, La Casa de las Américas, that decided which books would be published in Cuba.

against the outside wall of the house, and the stillness of the night conspired with the garden and the thickness of the wall to give him a sense of security, of peace almost, that he had not experienced for many years, too many years.... Alfredo would have preferred to remain there, outside the house, alone with his characters, listening to the music from far away. But, always keeping in mind the solid publishing project that would perhaps one day allow him to own a mansion like this one and that could also mean the future salvation of Olga, Daniel, Delfín, Berta, and Nicolás, he rang the doorbell.

Before one of the maids (hired specially for the reception) could open the door, an enormous Saint Bernard belonging to the Pérez Campos lunged toward him and began licking his face. This display of familiarity from the huge dog (which answered to the name of Narcisa) encouraged similar shows of affection from the other dogs, six Chihuahuas who welcomed Alfredo with a chorus of piercing barks. Fortunately, Gladys herself came to the rescue of her guest of honor.

Fashionably attired—although rather inappropriately for the climate—in an ankle-length skirt, boa, gloves, and a large hat, the hostess took Alfredo's arm and led him to the most select circle of guests, those who would also be most interested in the publishing venture. Gladys, at once solemn and festive, introduced him to the president of one of the city's most important banks (in his imagination Alfredo saw Berta making a face in disgust); to the executive vice president of the *Florida Herald,* the most influential newspaper in Miami ("A horrible, anti-Cuban paper," he heard Nicolás's voice saying from a distance); to the governor's personal assistant; and to an award-winning lady poet ("A couple of serious bitches," Delfín's sarcastic voice piped in loud and clear). The introductions continued: a distinguished minister who was a famous theology professor as well as the leader of the so-called Reunification of Cuban Families. ("What are you doing with these awful people?" Daniel shouted desperately from far away, causing Alfredo to trip just as he reached out for a famous opera singer's hand, and fall instead directly into the diva's ample bosom.) Gladys continued with her introductions as if nothing had happened: a famous woman pianist, two guitarists, several professors, and finally (here Gladys assumed a regal bearing), the Countess of Villalta. Born in the province of Pinar del Río, she was an elderly woman, no longer in possession of lands and villas, but still holding fast to her splendid title of nobility.

As he was on the point of bowing discreetly before the countess, Alfredo sensed that the characters of his budding opus were again urgently demanding his attention. And so, as he kissed the lady's hand, he decided to search for the pen and paper that he always carried in his pocket, in the hope of being able to jot down a few notes. But the countess misconstrued his intentions.

"I sincerely appreciate your giving me your address," said the lady, "but, as I am sure you will understand, this is just not the right moment. I do promise to send you my card."

And with that, the countess turned to the award-winning poetess, who had witnessed the scene and, apparently trying to help Alfredo, offered a suggestion: "Now that you've almost finished writing your address, why don't you give it to me? I do want to send you my latest book."

And instead of taking notes as his characters demanded (by now Olga was moaning and Berta screaming), Alfredo had no choice but to write his address on the piece of paper.

Trays brimming with assorted cheeses, hors d'oeuvres, pastries, and drinks were being passed around. Trays that, amid new greetings and inquiries, Alfredo saw approach and then disappear without his ever having a chance to sample from them.

At midnight Gladys announced that, in order to make the gathering more intimate, they would all move to the glass tower. This elicited a very pleased "Aaah!" from the guests (even the countess joined in), and, led by their fashionable hostess, they set off immediately.

The glass tower, circular and transparent, rose at one side of the house like a gigantic chimney. While the guests climbed laboriously up the spiral staircase (except the countess, who was transported in a chair designed especially for this purpose), Alfredo again heard his characters' urgent cries. Imprisoned in Holguín, deep in the Cuban countryside, Delfín begged not to be forsaken; from New York, Daniel's groans sounded aggravated and menacing; from a small French village, Olga, sweet Olga with her pages still blank, looked at him with a combination of reproach and melancholy in her eyes; meanwhile Nicolás and Berta, right there in Miami, angrily demanded immediate participation in the narrative that he had still not begun. To appease them momentarily, Alfredo tried to raise his hand in a gesture of understanding, but, as he did this, he accidentally tousled the pianist's elaborate coiffure, and she in turn gave him an even more hateful look than Berta's.

By now they had all reached the glass tower. Alfredo was expecting the real conversation to begin at any moment; that is, they would finally start talking about the publishing plans and the first authors to be published. But just then, Gladys (who had changed into an even more sumptuous gown without anyone noticing) gestured with an elegant wave of her hand for the musicians to start playing. Soon the bank president was dancing with the wife of the executive vice president of the *Florida Herald,* who in turn began dancing with the governor's assistant. A college professor deftly whirled around the room in the strong arms of the opera singer, outclassed only by the celebrated poetess, who was now performing a prizewinning solo. Between the clicking of her heels and the frenetic undulations of her hips and shoulders, she careened over to Alfredo, who had no choice other than to join the dance.

When the music ended, Alfredo thought that the time had finally come to discuss the central issue of the gathering. But at another signal from Gladys, the orchestra struck up a dance number from Spain. And even the most reverend minister, in the arms of the old countess, dared to venture a few parsimonious steps. As the dancing continued and the operatic singer began to show off her high notes, Alfredo was sure he could hear quite distinctly the voices of his characters, now at very close range. Without interrupting his dance, he passed close by the glass wall and looked out into the garden, where he saw Olga, quivering desperately among the geraniums, begging to be rescued with silent gestures; farther away, by the perfectly trimmed ficus trees, Daniel was sobbing. At that moment, as the diva's notes reached a crescendo, Alfredo felt he could no longer excuse his own indolence and, still dancing, he grabbed a napkin in flight and began desperately to scribble some notes.

"What kind of a dance is this?" interrupted the executive

vice president of the *Florida Herald*. "Do you also keep a record of your dance steps?"

Alfredo didn't know what to say. On top of it all, the pianist's stare, suspicious and alert, made him feel even more vulnerable. Wiping his brow with the napkin, he lowered his eyes in embarrassment and tried to pull himself together, but when he looked up again, there they were, Nicolás, Berta, and Delfín, already pressing against the glass walls of the tower. Yes, they had gathered here from different places to pound on the windowpanes and demand that Alfredo admit them (infuse them with life) into the pages of the novel—or story— that he had not even begun to write.

The six Chihuahuas began barking excitedly, and Alfredo thought that they too had seen his characters. Fortunately, however, their barking was just one of Gladys's bright ideas (or "exquisite touches," as the countess called them) to entertain her guests. And entertain them she did when, following her steps and the beat of the orchestra drums, the Chihuahuas surrounded Narcisa the Saint Bernard, and, standing on their hind legs, imitated complicated dance steps with Narcisa herself as the central figure. For a moment Alfredo was sure he saw a sadness in the eyes of the huge Saint Bernard, as the dog looked over at him. Finally, the audience burst into applause, and the orchestra shifted to the soft rhythms of a Cuban *danzón*.

Berta, Nicolás, and Delfín were now pounding even harder on the windows, while Alfredo, becoming more and more exasperated, whirled around in the arms of the award-winning poetess, Señora Clara del Prado (haven't we mentioned her by name yet?), who at that moment was confessing to the writer how difficult it was to get a book of poetry published.

"I know exactly what you mean," Alfredo agreed mechanically, distracted by his characters, who were now struggling on the other side of the glass like huge insects drawn to a hermetically sealed street lamp.

"You couldn't possibly understand," he heard the poet's voice counter.

"Why not?"

By then, out in the garden, Daniel and Olga had begun sobbing in unison.

"Because you are a novelist and novels always sell more than poems, especially when the author is famous like you. . . ."

"Don't make me laugh."

By now Daniel's and Olga's sobs were no longer sobs at all but agonized screams that ended in a single, unanimous plea for help.

"Rescue us! Rescue us!"

"Come on," urged the celebrated poetess, "stop acting so modest and tell me, just between you and me, how much do you get a year in royalties?"

And as if the screams coming from the garden were not enough to drive anyone out of his mind, Nicolás and Berta were now trying to break through the glass walls of the tower, with Delfín's enthusiastic encouragement.

"Royalties? Don't make me laugh. Don't you know that there's no copyright law in Cuba? All my books were published in other countries, while I was still in Cuba."

"Rescue us, or we'll break down the door!" This was, without a doubt, Berta's infuriated voice.

"They're all thieves, I know that. But other countries don't have to abide by Cuban law."

With their bare hands, and then their feet, Berta and Nicolás were beating on the glass wall, while the screams coming from the garden grew louder and louder.

"Other countries will adopt any law that allows them to plunder with impunity," Alfredo asserted clearly, ready to abandon the poetess in order to save his characters, who seemed, strangely enough, to be gasping for air, although out in the open.

"So how are you planning to get funding for the great publishing house?" inquired the award-winning poetess, with an ingratiating twinkle, before adding in a conspiratorial tone: "Oh, come on, I'm not going to ask you for a loan. I only want to publish a little volume of mine. . . ."

Somehow—Alfredo could not figure out exactly how—Berta had managed to slip one hand through the glass, and right in front of her astonished creator, turned the lock and opened one of the tower windows.

"Look, lady," Alfredo said curtly, "the fact is I don't have any money. As far as the publishing house is concerned, I am here to find out how everyone here plans on establishing it and whether I can get my books published, too."

"We've all been told that you are going to be the backer."

At that moment, Delfín slid down the tower and was now hanging dangerously by his fingers from the edge of the open window.

"Watch out!" Alfredo screamed, looking toward the window and trying to avert his character's fall.

"I thought we poets were the only crazy ones," said the

lady poet, staring intently at Alfredo, "but now I see that nov-elists are too—perhaps twice as crazy."

"Three times as crazy!" proclaimed Alfredo, running to Delfín's aid at the window, just as Berta González and Nicolás Landrove entered the room.

Alfredo felt embarrassed to have Nicolás, Berta, and Delfín Prats (whose life he had just saved) see him surrounded by all these people instead of being at work with them; there-fore, feeling more and more under pressure to remove himself and his characters from the scene, he decided to say good-bye to his hostess and to the rest of the guests instead of waiting for the famous discussion to begin. Followed by Narcisa, who was now intent on sniffing his leg, he walked over to them.

But a strange tension permeated the tower. Suddenly nobody was paying any attention to Alfredo. Worse, he seemed to have become invisible. In her tinkling tones, the celebrated poetess had just communicated something to Gladys and her friends, and they all made faces as if surprised or offended. Alfredo did not need a writer's observational skills to realize that they were talking about him, and not favorably.

"He'd better leave!" he heard Gladys Pérez Campo mut-ter in a low, indignant voice.

But even if he understood (albeit with some measure of surprise) that those words referred to him, Alfredo felt so con-fused that he was not able to absorb them. Besides, the words had not been spoken directly to him, although they were cer-tainly intended for his ears. Gladys's good manners and social standing would not allow her to make a public scene, much less force one of her guests to leave. Therefore, still with the intention of rescuing his characters (who were now, for their part, completely ignoring him), Alfredo pretended not to have noticed and tried to blend in with the conversation. But the countess gave him a look of such withering scorn that the confused writer took refuge in a corner and lit a cigarette. But wouldn't it be a sign of very poor breeding to leave without saying good-bye to the host and the other guests?

On top of everything else, right at that moment Delfín Prats opened the door to the spiral staircase, and Daniel Fernández and Olga Neshein came in. Holding hands and without even looking at Alfredo, they joined Nicolás Landrove and Berta González del Valle, both of whom had already had a few drinks and were well on their way to getting drunk. Once again Alfredo felt Narcisa's tail brushing against his legs.

The five characters of his story (by now, at least, he knew that these people were worth only a story) took great pleasure in walking around the room, eyeing everything with a mixture of curiosity and calculation. Alfredo concentrated all his energy on trying to make them leave. But they just would not obey. On the contrary, they mingled with the most prominent of the guests, the true elite, introducing themselves to one another, bowing and curtseying, and exchanging pleasantries.

From the corner where he was hidden behind a huge tropical palm and obscured by the smoke from his cigarette, Alfredo carefully observed his five characters and discovered that none was dressed as he had decided. Olga, supposedly shy and sweet, had arrived wearing too much makeup and a tight miniskirt; she was gesticulating wildly, making faces and laughing too hard at a joke that the director of Reunification of Cuban Families had just told her. Meanwhile, Berta and Nicolás, the paragons of "unshakable integrity," according to

Alfredo's vision of them, were kowtowing outrageously to the governor's assistant. At one point, Alfredo even thought he overheard them asking for a small business loan to open a pizzeria in the center of the city. For his part, Daniel ("the introverted, solitary one") had already introduced himself as Daniel Fernández Trujillo and was telling the award-winning poetess such off-color stories that the old countess had discreetly moved to another seat. But the insolence seemed to have met its master in the talented Delfín Prats Pupo. While downing a beer (his fifth? his seventh?) straight from the bottle, he mocked his creator—that is, Alfredo Fuentes—in a manner that was not only grotesque, but also almost obscene and ruthless. With diabolical skill, Delfín Prats Pupo imitated Alfredo, exaggerating all of the writer's tics, gestures, and idiosyncrasies, including his manner of speaking, walking, and even breathing. Only then did Alfredo realize that he sometimes stammered, that he walked with his stomach thrust forward, and that he was bug-eyed. And as he watched his favorite character mock him, he also had to endure more face-licking from the passionate Saint Bernard.

"The worst thing of all is that for all his pretensions and ridiculous posturing as a brilliant author, he has no talent whatsoever and can't even write without making spelling mistakes. He often misspells my first family name and writes it without the *t*," concluded Delfín Prats Pupo, so as not to leave any doubt on the matter.

And everyone laughed, again producing a strange sound like the tinkling of wineglasses.

Increasingly nervous, Alfredo lit another cigarette, which he quickly dropped on the floor when Delfín Prats Pupo, mimicking his every gesture, began to light one too.

"Sir, would you please pick up that butt?" one of the nearest servants reprimanded him. "Or are you trying to burn the carpet?"

Alfredo bent down to do as he was told, and, while in that position, verified that the peculiar tinkling sound was produced by the tittering voices of the guests as they whispered, glancing at him with contempt. He brusquely extricated himself from the Saint Bernard's legs, as the dog howled pitifully, and approached the guests to try to figure out what was going on. But as soon as he joined the group, the governor's assistant, without looking at him, announced her immediate departure.

Suddenly, as if propelled by a spring, the guests decided that it was time to leave. The countess was carried away in her imposing chair, while most of the guests kissed her hand, which was now transparent (at least to Alfredo). The famous opera singer was also leaving, on the (truly transparent) arm of the bank president. The minister turned to go while keeping up a lively conversation with the pianist, whose face was becoming more and more shiny and brilliant. When the award-winning lady poet left with Daniel Fernández Trujillo's arm around her waist, Alfredo saw the young man's hand sink effortlessly into her translucent body (although Daniel Fernández Trujillo's hand soon became invisible as well, and both figures fused into one). The black musicians were also leaving, led by Delfín Prats Pupo, who jumped around among them cheerfully, producing the familiar tinkling sound, while mimicking the gestures of the writer, who could do nothing to stop him. Olga Neshein de Leviant left with a mathematics professor, their hands entwined. In the midst of this stampede, Berta González del Valle stuffed her handbag with French cheeses, and Nicolás Landrove Felipe carted away the candy, both of them oblivious to Alfredo's signals and the protests of the hostess, Gladys Pérez Campo, who, on her way out in the company of her Chihuahuas, threatened to call the police. But her voice faded away into an imperceptible tinkling.

Within a few minutes, the hostess, the guests, and even the hired staff had disappeared, along with the characters of the story, and Alfredo found himself alone in the huge mansion. Disconcerted, he was getting ready to leave when the thunder of trucks and cranes reverberated through the building.

Suddenly the foundations of the house began to move and the roof disappeared; the carpets rolled up automatically; the windowpanes, freed from their casements, flew through the air; the doors left their frames; the paintings came off the walls; and the walls, moving at an unbelievable speed, vanished along with everything else, into a huge truck. As everything disassembled and packed itself (the whole garden with its plastic trees, walls, and air fresheners was already moving out), Alfredo saw that the mansion had been nothing more than an enormous prefabricated cardboard set that could be installed and dismantled quickly, and which one could rent for a few days or even a few hours, according to the ad on the side of the large truck in which everything was being carted away.

In a flash, the site where the imposing mansion had stood became nothing but a dusty embankment. Standing in the center, still perplexed, Alfredo could not find (it no longer existed) the path that would take him back to the city. He walked around aimlessly, thinking about the story he had never written. But an enthusiastic bark pulled him out of his meditation.

Exasperated, Alfredo began running, but the Saint Bernard, evidently more athletic than the writer, caught up with him quickly, knocked him down, and began licking his face. An unexpected joy came over Alfredo when he realized that her tongue was indeed real. He pulled himself together and got up. Caressing Narcisa—who followed him faithfully—he abandoned the site.

Miami Beach, April 1986

With My Eyes Closed

I'M ONLY GOING to tell the whole story to you because I know that if I tell it to you, you're not going to laugh in my face and you're not going to scold me either. I can't tell my mother. I can't tell Mother anything, 'cause if I did, she would never stop nagging and scolding me. And, even though she would probably be right, I really don't want to hear any kind of warning or advice.

So that's why. Because I know you're not going to say anything to me, I'm telling you all.

Since I'm only eight, I go to school every day. And that is when all my troubles start, 'cause I have to get up pretty early—when the bantam rooster my grandaunt Angela gave me has only crowed twice. My school is pretty far.

About six in the morning my mother begins scolding me for not getting up, and by seven I'm already sitting on the bed and rubbing my eyes. Then I have to do everything in a hurry: get dressed fast, run fast to school, and get in line fast because the bell rang already and the teacher is standing by the door.

But yesterday was different. My grandaunt Angela had to leave for Oriente and catch a train before seven. And there was a tremendous racket around the house. All the neighbors came to say good-bye, and my mother got so nervous that she dropped the pot of boiling water for making coffee on the floor, and burned her foot.

With all that unbearable noise, I couldn't sleep any more. And since I was already awake, I decided to get up.

Grandaunt Angela, after a lot of hugs and kisses, finally managed to go. And I left right away for school, even though it was still pretty early.

Today I don't have to rush, I told myself, almost smiling. In fact, I began walking pretty slowly. And when I was going to cross the street, I stumbled over a cat lying on the curb. "What a place you picked to sleep," I told him, and I nudged him with the tip of my shoe. But he didn't move. Then I bent down closer and realized he was dead. Poor thing, I thought, he was probably run over by a car and someone dragged him over to the curbside so he wouldn't get totally squashed. What a shame. He was a big yellow cat who surely did not want to die. Anyway, it's too late now. And I kept on walking.

As it was still early, I stopped by the pastry shop. It's far from school, but it always has freshly baked, delicious pastries. There are two old ladies always standing by the door of the shop, each one carrying a shopping bag and asking for charity, hand extended. One day I gave each lady a nickel, and they both said at the same time, "May God bless your soul." That really made me laugh, so I grabbed two more nickels to put in their awfully wrinkled, freckly hands. Again they said together, "May God bless your soul," but by that time I didn't feel like laughing anymore. And since then, every time I walk by, these wrinkled black women give me a knowing look, and I can't help but give each one a nickel. Except yesterday: I really couldn't give them anything 'cause I had already spent the whole quarter I have for my afternoon snack on chocolate cookies. I had to leave through the back door so they wouldn't see me.

I only needed then to get across the bridge and walk two more blocks to school.

I stopped at the bridge for a moment because I heard a lot of noise below by the river's edge. I leaned as far as possible over the railing in order to be able to see. A group of boys of all ages had trapped a water rat in a corner and were throwing rocks and hollering at it. The rat was running from one side of the corner to the other and squealing sharply in desperation: it had no escape. Finally one of the boys took a bamboo pole and hit it on the back with all his might, squashing it. After the others ran to it, jumping up and down with the joy of victory, one of them picked up the body and hurled it into the middle of the river. The dead rat did not sink. It floated on its back for a while until it disappeared under the current.

The boys kept on shouting and moved to another part of the river. I started walking also.

Gosh, I told myself, it's so easy to walk over the bridge. I can even do it with my eyes closed. There is a railing to prevent you from falling in the water on one side and, on the other, the edge of the curb warns you not to step on the road. And to prove it, I closed my eyes and kept walking. At first I held on to the bridge railing with one hand, but after a while I didn't need to. And I kept walking with my eyes closed. And don't you go and tell it to my mother, but with your eyes closed there are many things you can see, even better than when you keep them open. The first thing I saw was a big yellowish cloud that sometimes shone more brightly than others, just like the sun when it's filtering through the trees. Then I closed my eyes really tight and the reddish cloud turned blue. And not only blue, but green. Green, then purple. Bright purple, like a rainbow that comes out after it has rained a lot and the earth is almost drowning.

And, with my eyes closed, I began thinking about the streets and about other things, and I kept on walking without stopping. And I saw my grandaunt Angela as she was leaving the house. Except she wasn't in the red polka-dot dress that she always wears when she goes to Oriente but in a long, white dress. And being so tall, she was like a telephone pole wrapped in a bedsheet. But she looked fine.

And I kept walking. I stumbled again over the cat on the curb. But this time, when I touched him with the tip of my shoe, he jumped up and ran away. The bright yellow cat ran away because he was alive and got scared when I woke him up. And I laughed a lot when I saw him vanish like a tornado, his back arched, his hair bristling with electricity.

I kept walking, with my eyes closed tight, of course. And that's how I got back to the pastry shop. Since I couldn't buy any pastries for myself because I had already spent all my food money, I could only look at the ones in the shop window. And I was just doing that, looking at them, when I heard two voices behind the counter asking me, "Wouldn't you like one of these?" And when I looked up, I saw that the two old ladies who were always begging at the shop entrance now seemed to be working there. I didn't know what to say. But their guess was exactly right, and full of smiles they picked up a large, reddish chocolate-almond cake. And they gave it to me.

I went crazy with joy and walked away with my huge cake.

While crossing the bridge, carrying the cake in my hands, I again heard the ruckus of the noisy boys. And (with my eyes closed) I leaned over the bridge railing and saw them down below, swimming fast toward the middle of the river in order to rescue a water rat. The poor thing looked sick and couldn't swim.

The boys took the trembling rat out of the water and put it on top of a rock on the sandy shore so it could get dry in the sun. Then I was just about to call all of them over to join me and share the chocolate cake, because it was so big that I wouldn't be able to eat it all by myself.

I swear I was going to call them. And I lifted the cake up high for them to see, so that they would believe what I was about to tell them and come running. But then, pow!, a truck almost ran over me in the middle of the street, which is where, without realizing it, I had been standing.

So here I am: my legs are all white because of the casts and the bandages. As white as the walls in this room, with only women dressed in white coming in to give me an injection or a pill, also white.

And don't you think that what I told you is made up. And don't you think, just because I have a bit of a fever and every once in a while I complain about the pain in my legs, that I am lying to you, because it's not so. And if you want to see if what I told you is true, you only need to go to the bridge and you'll probably find, all over the asphalt, the big, reddish chocolate-almond cake that the two old ladies at the pastry shop gave me with a smile.

1964

The Great Force

WHEN THE GREAT FORCE CREATED everything that is, she did also create the human race. But the moment she got an inkling of her creatures' behavior—this required only a few hours—she ascended in terror back to the heavens, fearing for her own existence. Once reinstalled at the zenith, she proceeded with her diverse creations, including her masterpiece or, at least, what she considered to be her masterpiece. A perfect being that would reflect her and honor her: a son. In a state of powerful plenitude, the Great Force shared a few years with her closest kin, and almost forgot the lowly ones, or terrestrials, as humans were referred to in her court, and the remote place they inhabited. She could not, however, keep her son from finding out about her flawed creation, much less prevent (given the nature of children) his harboring the wish to descend for a visit, and even to converse with the denizens of the abominable region. The stronger and more irrefutable were the Great Force's arguments about the evil nature of the lowly ones, the greater was the son's interest in getting to know them and attempting to reform their ways. In addition to this, there were the incentives applied by the closest friends of the Great Force to encourage the son (and let's not talk about her enemies, who pictured the planet as paradise itself). It was then quite understandable that within a few months the son finally made his descent to Earth. After a lengthy journey through numerous galaxies, the son arrived at the long-anticipated location, where what he saw was a teeming anthill voraciously feeding on itself. Naturally, said the son (who always knew the appropriate answers to everything), they are trying to find themselves, and not succeeding. I will show them who they are, so that instead of destroying one another, they will be filled with brotherly love. . . . Once on Earth, without much ado the son commenced his teachings about self-knowledge and brotherly love, which unleashed an even greater violence and hatred than those beings had ever experienced. The conservatives considered such teachings an insult to established morality; the liberals attacked the son as reactionary, for not practicing violence. The powerful feared their position was being threatened, and the poor imagined that the whole issue was nothing but a ruse devised to enhance even further their thralldom to the powerful. As for the envious ones, which amounted to nearly the whole population, they flatly rejected him outright, simply because they could not tolerate having anyone outshine them. And so it happened that as soon as the son was able to realize his predicament and cry out for his progenitor's help, he was quickly torn to pieces. But the Great Force (as any force would do) revived her son, and in his rescue made him soar at lightning speed through the heavens. The commotion this produced on Earth was felt unanimously. Executioners and their accomplices, that is, the whole human race, fell to their knees and began worshiping the disappearing figure. Since that moment they trustfully await, amid crass injustices and flagellations, the one who will bring them redemption. But now the son is far from being the slender, long-haired youth who in order to assert himself had to disobey his parent. As owner of a gigantic nebula, he raises phosphorescent asteroids; he has lost most of his hair, and has numerous, beautiful offspring (the pride and joy of the Great Force, somewhat mellowed over the years) who are forbidden to learn about astronomy. Besides, the son no longer remembers where the earth is located, and does not even remotely intend to pay it a visit.

"That is what the foolish narrator of this story believes. I am actually watching closely for the slightest opportunity to escape this realm and make my second descent."

New York, 1987

Mona

To Delfín Prats,
my loyal reader during the seventies

I am fully conscious that not being a man. . . .
LEONARDO DA VINCI
Notebooks

Foreword
by Daniel Sakuntala

A PECULIAR BIT OF NEWS APPEARED in the international press in October of 1986. Ramón Fernández, twenty-seven, who had come to the United States in the Mariel exodus from Cuba, was arrested at the Metropolitan Museum of Art as he "attempted to knife" the Mona Lisa, Leonardo da Vinci's famous painting, valued at a hundred million dollars.

Most of the newspaper reports offered basic information on the artist and his masterpiece, then speculated that Mr. Fernández was one of the many mental patients who were expelled from Cuba in the 1980 Mariel boatlift. The museum's exhibit of the famous painting would be extended until the fifteenth of November 1986, by special permission from the Louvre. That was all they said, and whether it was for reasons of diplomacy or out of ignorance they omitted a minor detail: Mitterrand's French government would pocket five million dollars for the "courtesy" of having allowed the Mona Lisa to cross the Atlantic. It is interesting to note that the press— especially that in the United States—emphasized the fact that the suspect, a presumed mental case, was a *marielito.* Also of interest is the media's reference to an attempt to knife the painting, when according to all the evidence, including the suspect's confession, the assault weapon was a hammer. . . . A few days later, on October 17, the *New York Times,* deep in one of its back pages, printed a brief account of the strange death of the detainee Ramón Fernández: "The young man from Cuba who attempted to destroy Leonardo da Vinci's master-piece was found strangled in his prison cell this morning. He had been waiting to make his first court appearance. Oddly," the reporter added, "the suicide weapon is still a mystery." Aware of the detainee's mental condition, the authorities had deprived him of his belt and shoelaces. The prisoner seemed to have strangled himself with his bare hands. No one from the outside had visited Mr. Fernández, who, according to the war-den, had spent his six days of incarceration in a highly agitated state, writing what appeared to be a long letter—which he subsequently mailed to one of his Cuban friends in exile. The warden declared that because this was a special case, he had taken the precaution of reading this document (obtained through a policeman who had pretended to befriend Mr. Fer-nández), and it confirmed the inmate's state of extreme mental disturbance. After photocopying the letter, he had it mailed to its addressee, "since it added nothing (sic) to the evidence." Two days later, while the front pages gave coverage to Mother Teresa's suicide, only a few newspapers reported that Ramón

Fernández's body had mysteriously disappeared from the morgue, where it was awaiting the arrival of the forensic physician and the district attorney. Thus ends the more or less hard news regarding the case, news that began with a confused bit of information (the so-called knifing of the Mona Lisa) and ended similarly (with the apparent suicide of the suspect). In the confident wisdom so characteristic of ignorance, the yellow press sniffed a crime of passion behind all this. . . . Needless to say, a flock of magazines and New York tabloids—those called liberal because they are ready to defend any enemy empire against the American empire—headed by the *Village Voice,* reported the events differently: Ramón Fernández was an anti-Castro Cuban terrorist who, in clear opposition to the socialist French government, had attempted to destroy that country's most treasured work of art. And as if this were not enough to grant us Cubans the status of troglodytes, a libelous Hispanic rag published in New Jersey and funded by a Cuban extremist, Luis P. Suardíaz, wrote a blazing editorial in praise of Fernández's "patriotic deed," saying that his "action" had served to draw the French government's attention to the case of Roberto Bofill, a Cuban who had gained political asylum in the French embassy in Havana and had repeatedly been denied an exit permit by Fidel Castro.

Six months have passed since the mysterious death of Ramón Fernández. *La Gioconda* has returned to her home in the Louvre. The case appears to be closed.

There is someone, however, who won't easily accept the hasty closing of this case, particularly after twice having had the privilege of gracing the pages of the *New York Times,* as well as being published in several other journals. That person is none other than the author of these lines, Daniel Sakuntala, the recipient of the long testimony produced by Ramón Fernández. The police handed it to me, a week after Ramón's death, in an attempt to find out if there had been any compromising or murky dealings between the "suicide suspect" and myself. They intended to watch my reactions and follow my every step, and I am sure they did.

As soon as I received the manuscript from my friend Ramoncito, whom I had met in Cuba, I tried to publish it in a serious newspaper or magazine, but all the editors agreed with the dull-witted police, saying that this testimony was the product of a hallucinating or deranged mind and that anyone who dared publish it would be ridiculed. Since I found no serious publication willing to make the text known, I contacted Reinaldo Arenas, as a last resort, to see if he would print it in his magazine, *Mariel.* But Arenas, with his proverbial frivolity* and in spite of the fact that he was already very sick with AIDS, the cause of his recent death, laughed at my suggestion, saying that *Mariel* was a modern magazine in which there was no room for this "nineteenth-century tale." To compound the insult, he told me to take it to the director of *Linden Lane Magazine,* Carilda Oliver Labra. . . . My guess is that Reinaldo had met Ramoncito in Cuba, and Ramoncito, who was attracted only to real women, had completely ignored Reinaldo. But that is another story, which reminds me of the time when Ramoncito, my friend and brother, slapped Delfín

Besides being frivolous, Arenas was a real ignoramus. As evidence of this, let me point out that in his short story "End of a Story," he mentions a statue of Jupiter atop the Chamber of Commerce in Havana, when everybody knows that crowning the cupola of that building is a statue of the god Mercury. —D. S.

Proust in a crowded bus in Havana because Delfín had suddenly grabbed at his fly. . . . Well, no respectable publication
was willing to print my friend's desperate testimony. Perhaps
if it had been taken seriously from the start, his life would have
been saved.

Since I hope it will save the lives of many other young and
handsome men, such as he was, I am taking it upon myself to
promulgate this document, using all the means at my disposal.
Here is the text, with only a few clarifying notes added. I sincerely hope that someone, someday, will take it seriously.

DANIEL SAKUNTALA
New York, 1987

Editors' Note

Before presenting this testimony by Ramón Fernández, it
seems advisable to clarify a few points. Daniel Sakuntala was
unable to publish this document during his lifetime in spite
of tenacious efforts. In the end, it seems that his economic
situation prevented him. We have a copy of a letter from Editorial Playor, asking two thousand dollars in advance for
the "printing of the booklet." The text was published in
New Jersey more than twenty-five years ago, in November
1999, after Mr. Sakuntala's mysterious disappearance (the
body was never found) near Lake Ontario. The publishers
were Ismaele Lorenzo and Vicente Echurre, the editors
then of the magazine *Unveiling Cuba*—who themselves have
recently also disappeared, together with most of the copies of
the book. (Unconfirmed rumors indicate that these senior citizens returned to Cuba after the invasion of Havana by Jamaica
in alliance with other Caribbean islands and, of course, Great

Britain.) As for Reinaldo Arenas, mentioned by Mr. Sakuntala, he was a writer of the 1960s generation, justly forgotten in our century. He died of AIDS in the summer of 1987 in New York.

Because of the number of printing errors in the first edition of this document and then its near disappearance, we are proud to present this edition as the true first edition. For that reason, we have left unchanged Ramón Fernández's idiosyncratic expressions, as well as Daniel Sakuntala's notes and those of Messrs. Lorenzo and Echurre, even though by now they may seem (or be) anachronistic or irrelevant.

Monterey, California, May 2025

Ramón Fernández's Testimony

This report is being written in a rush, and even so, I am afraid I won't be able to finish it. She knows where I am and any moment now will come to destroy me. I am saying *she,* and perhaps I should say *he,* though I don't know what to call *that thing.* From the beginning, she (or he?) ensnared me, confused me, and now is even trying to prevent me from writing this statement. But I must do it; I must do it, and in the clearest way possible. If I can finish it and someone reads it and believes it, perhaps I could still be saved. The authorities in this prison are certainly not going to do anything for me. That I know very well. When I told them that I needed not to be left alone, that I wanted them to lock me up and have someone watch over me day and night, they broke up laughing. "You're not important enough to deserve special security," they said. "But don't you worry, you won't be able to get out of this place anyway." "My problem is not that I want to get out," I told them. "What worries me is that someone might be able to get in. . . ." "Get in? Here no one gets in of his own free will, and you'd better be quiet unless you want us to put you to sleep right now." I was going to insist, but before opening my mouth again, I looked at one of the officers and saw in his eyes that sneering attitude of a free human being who looks down upon a madman, an imprisoned one at that. And I realized they were not going to listen to me.

The only thing left for me to do is to write, to describe the events, to write the whole thing up quickly and in a logical manner, as logical as my situation allows, and see if someone finally believes me and I am saved, though that is very unlikely.

Since I came to New York—and that was more than six years ago—I have worked as a security guard at the Wendy's on Broadway between 42nd and 43rd streets. It is open twenty-four hours a day, and since I had the night shift, my job was always very lively, dealing with many different kinds of people. Without overlooking my responsibilities, I had the opportunity to meet many women who came in for a snack or who just passed by, and from my post behind the glass wall and in my well-pressed and gold-braided uniform, I beckoned them in. Of course, not all of them took the bait, but many did. I want to make very clear that I am not bragging. One night, in just one shift, I managed to have three women (not including the Wendy's cashier, a very solid black woman I made it with in the ladies' room). The trouble came at quitting time: the three of them were waiting for me. I managed somehow, but this is no time to go into it. I left with the one I liked best, though I was really sorry I had to give up the other two. I have no family in this country, and all my lovers and even friends have been these nameless women whom I spotted while at my post at Wendy's or who (and I say this without any false modesty) spotted me and came in with the pretext of having a cup of tea or something.

One night I was on the alert, watching the street and looking for a woman worthy of a wink, when a truly extraordinary female specimen stopped outside. Long reddish hair, ample forehead, perfect nose, fine lips, and honey-colored eyes that looked me over openly (a bit shamelessly) through long false eyelashes. I must confess, she struck me instantly. I straightened my uniform jacket and took a good look at her body, which even under bulky winter clothes promised to be as extraordinary as her face. I was fascinated. Meanwhile, she came in, took off the stole or cape she had around her shoulders, and uncovered part of her breasts. That same night we agreed to meet at three o'clock in the morning, when I finished my shift.

She told me her name was Elisa, that she was of Greek ancestry, and that she was in New York for just a few weeks. This was enough for me to invite her to my room on 43rd Street, on the West Side, only three blocks away. Elisa accepted without hesitation, which pleased me enormously because I don't like women who play hard-to-get before going to bed with you. These are the ones who later, when you want to get rid of them, make your life unbearable. Since I didn't want to have that kind of trouble at Wendy's, I stayed away from these kinds of "difficult" women, who later, when you are not interested anymore, become quite a nuisance, capable of following you all the way to Siberia if necessary.

But with Elisa—let's keep calling her Elisa—that was no problem. From the start, she laid her cards on the table. She obviously liked me and wanted to go to bed with me often before returning to Europe. So I did not ask her any more personal questions (if you want to have a good time with a woman, never ask her about her life). We went to bed, and I must confess that in spite of all my experience, Elisa surprised me. She possessed not only the imagination of a real pleasure-seeker and the skills of a woman of the world but also a kind of motherly charm mixed with youthful mischief and the airs of a grand lady, which made her irresistible. Never had I enjoyed a woman so much.

I noted nothing strange in her that night, except for a peculiar pronunciation of certain words and phrases. For instance, she would begin a word in a very soft, feminine tone and end it in a heavy voice, almost masculine. I supposed it was due to her lack of knowledge of the Spanish language, which she adamantly insisted on speaking after I told her I was Cuban, though I had proposed, for her convenience, that we speak English. I could not help but laugh when she told me (perhaps to empathize with my Caribbean origins) that she had been born near the Mediterranean. I laughed not because being born there was funnier than having come into this world somewhere else but because she pronounced each syllable of the word *Mediterráneo* in a different voice. It seemed you were listening not to one woman but to five, each different from the other. When I pointed this out, I noticed that her beautiful forehead wrinkled.

Next day was my day off, and at dinnertime she suggested going to Plum's, an elegant restaurant that did not concur with the state of my wallet. I informed her of that fact, and she, looking at me intently but with bit of mockery, invited me to be her guest. I accepted.

At the restaurant that evening, Elisa did something that

puzzled me. The waiter, in this fancy place, forgot to bring us water. I signaled him several times. The man would promise it right away, but the water was not forthcoming. Unexpectedly, Elisa grabbed the vase adorning our table, removed the flowers, and drank the water. She quickly replaced the flowers and continued our conversation. She did this so naturally that anyone would have thought that drinking the water from a flower vase was the normal thing to do.... After dinner we went back to my room, and I enjoyed again, even more than before, the pleasures of her incredible body. At dawn, half-asleep, we were still kissing. I remember at one point the strange sensation of having close to my lips the thick underlip of some animal and quickly turned the light on. Next to mine, fortunately, I had only the lips of the most beautiful woman I had ever met. So fascinated was I with Elisa that I accepted her idea of my not going to Wendy's that night, which was a Monday. She claimed that it was the only day in the week that she could spend with me, and proposed taking a ride on my motorcycle (a 1981 Yamaha) out of the city. Across the Hudson, on the New Jersey side, Elisa asked me to stop for a look at the New York skyline. I knew that for a foreigner (and a tourist, given her carefree manner), the panoramic view of Manhattan, its towers like sierras, today mysteriously disappearing in fog, had to be impressive. Even I, so used to this panorama that I seldom took the time to look at it anymore, felt the enchantment of the view and seemed to perceive an intense glow radiating from the tallest buildings. This was rather strange, since at that time, close to eleven in the morning, the skyscrapers had no reason to be lit. I turned to tell Elisa, but she, leaning on the railing, facing the river, was not listening to me: she was as if transported, looking at the strange luminosity and muttering unintelligible words that I assumed were in her mother tongue. To bring her back from her soliloquy, I approached her from behind and put my hands on her shoulders, which were covered by a heavy woolen stole. A chill ran down my spine. One of her shoulders seemed to bulge out sharply, as if the bone were out of joint and in the shape of a hook. To make sure there was a deformity that inexplicably I had not discovered until then, I felt her shoulder again. There was no deformity, however, and through the fabric my hand caressed her warm, smooth skin. Then I thought that surely I must have touched a safety pin or a shoulder pad, now back in place. At that moment Elisa turned to me and said that we could go on whenever I wished.

We got on the motorcycle, but I couldn't get it to start. I inspected it carefully and finally told Elisa that I thought we could not continue our trip. My cycle had finally given out, and it would be better if we left it right there and took a taxi back to Manhattan. Elisa wanted to examine the motor herself. "I know about these things," she explained with a smile. "In my country I have a Lambretta"—that's what she said—"which is similar to this." Mistrusting her mechanical skills, I stepped aside to the lookout on the Hudson and lit a cigarette. I had no time to finish it. Giving its characteristic explosion, the starting motor began to roar.

Elated, we dashed off. Elisa suggested we take I-95 North to a little mountain town near the route to Buffalo. The higher we climbed, the more radiant the autumn noon became. The trees, deep crimson, appeared to be on fire. The fog had dissipated, and a warmish glow seemed to envelop everything. I kept glancing at Elisa in the rearview mirror; she had an expression of sweet serenity. It gave me such pleasure to see her like this, with her look of mysterious abandon, her face against the forest background, that I kept watching her in the little mirror, spellbound. Once, instead of her face, I thought I saw the face of a horrible old man, but I attributed this to our speed, which distorted images. . . . During the afternoon, we reached the mountains, and before dark we stopped at a town on a hill, with one- and two-story houses. More than a town, it looked like a promontory of whitewashed stones, above which rose a pure white church steeple so old that it did not seem to belong in America. Elisa cleared up the mystery for me. The town had been founded in the eighteenth century by a group of European immigrants (Spaniards and Italians), who chose such a remote location in order to be able to hold on to their old traditions. They were peasant folk, and according to Elisa, though they had arrived in 1760, they were still living as if in the Middle Ages. And it was indeed a small medieval city, despite its electricity and running water, and its location on the foothills of a New York mountain.*

Obviously the city Ramoncito refers to is Syracuse, in northern New York state. It's named for Siracusa, port and province of Italy, the land of Archimedes and Theocritus, and location of a famous Greek theater. —D. S.

We strongly disagree with Mr. Sakuntala. After traveling throughout New York state, we have concluded that the city visited by Ramón Fernández and Elisa must have been Albany. Only that city has houses that look like "whitewashed stone" and is located in the foothills of a mountain. There is also an old church with an all-white steeple. —Ismaele Lorenzo and Vicente Echurre, 1999

We reject both Daniel Sakuntala's and Messrs. Lorenzo and Echurre's theories. The city must be no other than Ithaca, located on a mountain north of New York City. Notice that in his testimony, Mr. Fernández states: "More than a town, it looked like a promontory of whitewashed stones." That is what Ithaca is. The stones are the famous Cornell University, and the white tower that looks like a church is the gigantic pillar that supports the library clock. —Editors, 2025

I was not surprised at Elisa's knowledge of architecture and history. I have always thought that Europeans, simply by being Europeans, know more about the past than Americans do. Up to a point, if you allow me, they *are* the past.

The prison bell is ringing: it's dinnertime, and I run. There, among the inmates and their shouting, and in the midst of all the clatter of dishes and utensils, I feel more secure than here, alone in my cell. To urge myself on, I vow that right after dinner I will continue writing this report.

Now I am in the prison library. It is eleven P.M. I am thinking that if nothing had happened, I would now be at Wendy's in my blue uniform with gold braid, behind the glass wall, protected from the cold and inspecting with my clinical eye every woman who passes by. But I have no time for women now. I am imprisoned here for a crime I have not committed, but given my status as a *marielito,* it is the same as if I had. I am waiting here not for my sentence, which by now obviously does not worry me much, but for Elisa, who, as soon as she can, will come and kill me.

But let's go back a few days to the night we spent in that old mountain town so dear to Elisa. After walking around for a while, we entered a restaurant that looked like a Spanish inn, something like La Bodeguita del Medio—The Little Inn in the Middle of the Block—a popular restaurant in Havana, which I, as a native, was not allowed to visit, except once, when a tourist, a Frenchwoman, invited me. . . . Elisa knew the place well. She knew how to choose the best table and the best dishes on the menu. It was clear she felt completely at home. And her beauty seemed to grow by the minute. She also knew how to pick a hotel; small and comfortable, it looked like a guesthouse. We retired early and made love passionately. I confess that in spite of all my enthusiasm, Elisa was hard to please (What woman isn't!), but I have my ways, and in these matters I always have the last word—even if my companion is a great conversationalist. Yes, I think that by daybreak I had managed to satisfy her completely. She was resting peacefully by my side. Before turning off the light, I wanted to get my fill of that quiet serenity of hers. She had fallen asleep, but her eyes did not remain closed for long. Suddenly I saw them disappear. I screamed in order to wake myself up—I had to have been dreaming—and immediately I could see her eyes, looking at me intently. "I think I had a nightmare," I told her in apology, and embracing her, I said good night. But afterward I was barely able to sleep at all.

Before dawn, Elisa got up and, without making a sound, left the room. I stood behind the window curtains and watched her vanish in the glow of the morning mist, following a yellow path that disappeared among the trees. I decided to stay awake and wait for her, even though I tried to calm myself by thinking that it was natural for someone to get up before dawn and take a walk: a European custom, maybe. I remembered the Frenchwoman who took me to La Bodeguita del Medio: she used to get up at dawn, take a shower, and, still wet, throw herself into bed. . . . About an hour later, I heard Elisa push the door open—I pretended to be asleep. She seemed out of breath. She sat next to me at the edge of the bed and turned off the light. Protected by darkness, I opened my eyes slightly. Facing the early light, her back to me, was a beautiful naked woman who would, any minute now, snuggle into bed with me. Her bottom, her back, her shoulders, her neck, everything was perfect. Except that her perfect body had no head.

Since in the face of the most outlandish circumstances we always search for logical explanations, I rationalized what I had seen as purely an effect produced by the heavy fog usual in that place. Anyway, my instinct told me it was better to keep silent and close my eyes. I felt Elisa sliding into bed next to me. Her hand, with unerring skill, caressed my genitals. "Are you alseep?" she asked. I opened my eyes as if waking up from a deep sleep and saw, next to me, her perfectly serene, smiling face. The color of her hair seemed to have grown even more intense. She kept caressing me, and even though I could not dismiss my misgivings, we embraced until we were totally fulfilled.

I have already been imprisoned for three days, and I believe I don't have three more days to live. So I must hurry. . . . This morning I was again shouting that I didn't want to be left alone. By noon the prison psychiatrist was sent to see me. I let him know I was not interested and answered his questions curtly. Not only because I knew he would do nothing for me, since, unfortunately, I am not crazy, but also because his interview, his stupid questions, were a waste of time, a waste of the precious little time I have left and that I must use to finish this story, send it to a friend, and see if he can do anything. Though I doubt it, I must go on.

———

We were back in New York City by nine-thirty in the morning, truly record time. Elisa had kept asking me to go very fast because, she claimed, she had to be at the Greek consulate at ten. At a red light on Fifth Avenue, she suddenly leaped off and began to run, saying that she would come to see me the next day at Wendy's. And she did. She came around nine P.M. to tell me she would be waiting for me when I left work—that is, at three in the morning. This was our agreement. But with all I had seen, or thought I had seen, plus the attraction Elisa exerted on me (or should I call it love?), I concluded that, as a matter of life and death, I had to find out who this woman really was.

On the pretext of sharp stomach pains, I left Wendy's without bothering to take off my uniform, and cautiously began to follow Elisa rather closely. At Broadway and 44th, she made a phone call, then started walking toward the theater district. On 47th Street, someone, who evidently was waiting for her, opened the door of a limousine, and Elisa got in. I was only able to see a masculine hand helping her in. It was easy to get a taxi and follow the limo, which stopped at 172 East 89th Street. The chauffeur opened the door, and Elisa and her companion went into the apartment building. To keep warm, I waited inside a telephone booth. An hour later, that is, around ten-thirty, Elisa came out. With my experience, I could tell that she had enjoyed a long and satisfying sexual encounter. She looked at her watch and started walking toward Central Park. She reached 79th and approached a bench where a young man was sitting, obviously waiting for her. I thought (I am sure of it) that he was the person Elisa had phoned from Broadway. The dialogue now was as short as the phone call had been. Without any fuss, they disappeared into the shrub-bery. Unseen, I was able to watch how quickly and easily the pair coupled. Dry leaves crackled under their bodies, and their panting scared away the squirrels, which clambered up the trees, screeching loudly. The whole thing lasted about an hour and a half, since by twelve-thirty Elisa was taking a leisurely walk in the 42nd Street porno district. Boldly, without any shame, she would ogle the men who passed obviously looking for a woman or something like that. Farther down the street, Elisa stopped in front of a towering, handsome black man standing by the door of a peep show. I was not able to hear their conversation, of course, but it seemed that Elisa got straight to the point: in less than five minutes they were inside one of the booths at the peep show. They stayed locked up in there for more than half an hour. When they came out, the young black man seemed exhausted; Elisa was radiant. It was now two o'clock in the morning, and she was still cruising around the area. A few seconds later I saw her, accompanied by three jocks who looked like hillbillies, entering a booth at the Black Jack peep show. Fifteen minutes later, the door slammed open and she came out, looking quite pleased. I did not wait to see the men's faces. . . . When I saw Elisa (now with a Puerto Rican who looked very much like a pimp) go into another peep show, the one on 8th Avenue between 43rd and 44th, I realized that my "fiancée" would not come to me late that night, as she had promised. And in spite of what I had been witnessing, I could not but feel a sense of total loss. Elisa was the woman with whom I had fallen in love, for the first time. . . . But at quarter to three, she came out of the peep show and started walking toward Wendy's. To be with her once more, I obliterated everything I had seen and started running, so I'd be there, waiting, when she came. The cashier and the other employees were puzzled to see me taking my post behind the glass wall. Elisa was there in no time, and together we went to my room.

That night in bed she was extraordinarily demanding, more so than ever, which is saying a lot. In spite of my desire and my extensive experience, it was not easy to satisfy her. Though after the encounter I pretended to fall asleep, I did not sleep a wink. What I had seen had left me totally perplexed. Of course, I could not tell her I had spied on her, could not appear jealous, though in all truth I was. Actually, I did not think I had the right to demand fidelity from her, since at no point had we vowed to be faithful to each other.

It was close to nine o'clock in the morning when, while I pretended to be asleep, she woke up, dressed in silence, and went out without saying good-bye. But I was obsessed (though now I regret it) with following that woman and finding out where she lived, who she really was. . . . At 43rd and Eighth she took a taxi. I took another. While following her, nodding in my seat, I wondered if it was possible for Elisa to be on her way to another tryst. She was not. After such a turbulent night, Elisa seemed to want to find inner peace by looking at works of art. At least that is what I thought when I saw her get out of the taxi and hurriedly enter the Metropolitan Museum, just at the moment it was opening its doors. After paying for admission, I rushed inside the building and went up to the second floor, following the route she had taken. I watched her go into one of those large galleries, and right there, in front of my eyes, she disappeared. I looked for her for hours throughout the immense building, without any success. I did not skip any possible corner. I looked behind every statue, went around every amphora (there are some enormous ones) and even searched inside them. On one occasion I got lost among countless sarcophagi and centuries-old mummies, while calling Elisa's name out loud. Once out of that labyrinth, I found myself in a temple of the time of the Ptolemies (according to a placard)* seemingly floating in a pool. I searched everywhere in that enormous pile of stones, but Elisa was not there either. About three in the afternoon I went back to my room and threw myself on the bed.

I woke up at two in the morning. In a rush, I put on my

---

*It is only natural that Ramoncito, who is not used to museums, mixes themes, styles, and periods. The temple he refers to must be that of Ramses II, built at the height of his reign during the nineteenth dynasty, in 1305 B.C., to be exact. It is an enormous red granite mound, where anyone who is not an expert can get lost. —D. S.

The only portion of that temple in the Metropolitan Museum was a stone about six feet tall. It would be impossible for Ramón Fernández to penetrate it. He must have entered the temple of Debot, which is in fact set in an artificial lake to re-create the original natural setting on the Nile. —Vicente Echurre, 1999

I disagree with my colleague, Mr. Echurre. The temple he is referring to exists, but it is in Madrid. It has surely escaped his memory, and I have tried to refresh it but in vain. Since obviously I must dissent, we have decided to express our opinions individually, no matter how absurd that of my associate might seem. Mine, specifically, is this: the area Mr. Fernández reached in the Metropolitan Museum was the temple, supposedly, of Kantur, which once belonged to Queen Cleopatra and which in 1965, thanks to the efforts of President John F. Kennedy, UNESCO sold to the United States for twenty million dollars. It was discovered later that this transaction had been a fraudulent one (one of many) carried out in collusion with Mr. Kennedy. UNESCO had sent the original temple to their headquarters in the Soviet Union and a plastic replica to the United States. This highly flammable copy was the cause of the big fire in the Metropolitan Museum. It seems that someone had carelessly dropped a lighted cigarette butt on it. —Ismaele Lorenzo, 1999

The only Egyptian temple then in the Metropolitan Museum was that of Pernaabi, from the fifth dynasty, circa 2400 before the Common Era. —Editors, 2025

uniform and left for Wendy's. My boss, who had always been pretty decent to me, told me that this was no time to start working; it was almost time to leave. I detected a tinge of sadness in his voice when he informed me that the next time this happened I would be fired. I assured him there would be no next time, and I went back to my room. Elisa was waiting by the door. I was not even surprised that she had been able to enter my building, though the front door is always locked and only the tenants have keys. She said she had been at Wendy's several times and I was not there, so she decided to wait for me in my house. We went into my room, and perhaps because I had slept for hours or because I was afraid I would never see her again, I made love to her with renewed passion. Yes, that night, I believe, I was the clear victor. But how many duels—I sadly asked myself—had she fought today before coming to me? . . . At dawn, when I again started an attack, sliding over her naked body, I saw that Elisa had no breasts. I jumped to the edge of the bed, wondering whether this woman was driving me insane. As if sensing my anguish, she immediately pulled me over with her arms to her beautiful breasts.

As on the previous day, Elisa got up around nine, dressed quickly, and went out. Her destination was the same, the Metropolitan Museum. And again she disappeared in front of my eyes.

She did not come to see me at work Thursday or Friday. On Saturday I got up early, determined to find her. I must add that, independent of all the mystery surrounding her person, which fascinated me, I felt the urge to go to bed with her immediately.

I took a taxi to the Metropolitan. Evidently there was a relationship between Elisa and that building, and I thought it was sort of stupid of me not to have realized before that she must be a museum employee, which explained why she was so interested in getting there at ten o'clock, when the doors opened to the public. My mistake had been to search for her among the visitors instead of in the offices.

I searched for her everywhere. I inquired at the information desk and in the staff office. There was no employee named Elisa. Of course, the fact that she told me her name was Elisa did not mean that was really her name; quite the contrary, perhaps. Anyone who worked among so many valuable objects (which for me, by the way, didn't mean a thing) and carried on sexually as she did, had to take precautions.

So I tried to find her physically among the numerous women who worked at the museum. While I was looking over the female guards, I noticed in one room a large group representing many nationalities (Japanese, South Americans, Chinese, Indians, Germans) gathered around a painting, while several guards, almost shouting, were trying to prevent the taking of photographs. Maybe I can find Elisa among them, I thought, and pushed my way into the crowd. And in fact, there she was. Not among those taking the photos, nor among the guards warning that this was not permitted, but inside the very painting everyone was looking at. I got as close as the red cord that served as barrier between painting and public would allow. That woman, with her straight, dark reddish hair and perfect features, with one hand placed delicately over the other wrist, was smiling almost impudently, against a background that seemed to be a road leading to a misty lake. The woman was, without any doubt, Elisa. I thought then that the mystery had been solved: Elisa was a famous, exclusive artists' model. That was why it was so difficult to find her. At that moment she was probably posing for another painter, perhaps as good as the one who had made this perfect portrait of her.

Before asking one of the guards where I could find the model for the painting that so many people wanted to photograph, I got closer in order to see it in greater detail. Next to the frame, a small placard stated that it was painted in 1505 by one Leonardo da Vinci. Stunned, I backed up to take a good look at the canvas. My eyes then met Elisa's intense gaze in the painting. I held her gaze and discovered that Elisa's eyes had no eyelashes; she had the eyes of a serpent.

The prison bell is again announcing it is bedtime. I will have to continue this report tomorrow. I must rush, since I believe I have no more than two days left to live.

Of course, no matter how much the woman in the painting resembled Elisa, it was impossible for her to have been the model. So I quickly tried to find a reasonable explanation for the phenomenon. According to the small catalog at the gallery's entrance, the painting was valued at many millions of dollars (more than eighty million, the catalog read).* The woman in the picture (according to the same catalog) was

*It is interesting to note that the value of the painting according to the New York Times was about $100 million, while the catalog quoted $80 million. We believe this was a government trick to raise taxes for the right to exhibit that

European. And so was Elisa. The woman in the picture then could be one of Elisa's remote ancestors. Therefore Elisa could be the owner of that painting. And since it was so valuable, Elisa could travel with it for security reasons and would come and inspect it every morning. Then, after checking that nothing had happened to it during the night, which is the time when most thieves choose to operate, she would withdraw to another area of the museum. Now her pains to hide her identity seemed clear to me. She was a nymphomaniac millionaire who, for obvious reasons, had to keep her sexual relationships anonymous.

I have to admit I enjoyed the idea of being associated with a woman who had so many millions. Perhaps, if I played my cards right and pleased her in every way (and this was my heart's desire), Elisa would help me out and I could someday open my own Wendy's. In my enthusiasm I was forgetting the eccentricities and the imperfections, the defects, anomalies, or whatever you want to call them, that at certain moments I detected in her.

Now the only thing I had to do was to be pleasant, to allow no interest in money, and not to bother her with indiscreet questions. I bought a bunch of roses from a stand that, being on Fifth Avenue, charged me fifteen dollars, and I went to wait for Elisa at the front entrance of the museum, because if she was inside—and I was sure she was—sooner or later she

---

famous masterpiece in this country. This suspicion was almost absolutely confirmed in 1992 when it was disclosed, on the opening of former President Ronald Reagan's will, that he had owned the New York Times *since 1944. The anti-Republican sentiment of that newspaper (which after this scandal was forced to cease publication) was nothing but a political tactic to prevent suspicion.*
—Lorenzo and Echurre, 1999

would have to come out. But she did not. With my bunch of roses, I remained at my post, under a New York drizzle, until ten o'clock, when the museum closed on Fridays.*

When I got to Wendy's it was eleven P.M. I was three hours late. I was fired then and there. Before leaving, I gave the roses to the cashier.

After walking around Broadway until very late, I returned to my room in a state of depression. Elisa was there, waiting for me. As usual, she was elegantly dressed, and this time she was carrying a camera, a very expensive professional one. I invited her in and told her about my being fired. "Don't worry," she said. "With me on your side, you won't have any problem." And I believed her, thinking of her fortune, and so I asked her to get into bed with me. Because the first thing a man must do to keep on good terms with a woman is to invite her to his bed; even though she may not accept at the beginning, or maybe ever, she will always be grateful. . . . Strangely enough, she did not accept. She asked me to go to bed alone because she had to meditate ("concentrate," I remember now, is the exact word she used) on a project she had to work on the following day, Saturday—though since the sun was almost out, it was already Saturday.

I thought it was best to obey my future boss, and I went to bed alone, though, of course, I did not intend to sleep. Awake

*There must have been a special event that day at the museum, since it usually closes at ten only on Wednesdays. —D. S.

The Metropolitan Museum in New York closed at ten o'clock on Wednesdays and Fridays. Mr. Sakuntala's knowledge of these matters is neglible. —Lorenzo and Echurre, 1999

Before the big fire, the Metropolitan Museum was open Tuesdays and Sundays until ten o'clock. We hope that as soon as repairs are completed and the museum reopens, it will have the same schedule. —Editors, 2025

but snoring lightly, I observed her discreetly. She walked back and forth in my studio for over two hours while mumbling unintelligible gibberish. I could make out "the inventors . . . the interpreters" at one point. Though I am not even sure of that, for Elisa was talking faster and faster, and her pace seemed to keep rhythm with her words. Finally she took off her splendid dress and went out the window, naked, onto the fire escape. With her hands uplifted and her head tilted back, as if in position to receive an extraordinary gift from the skies (now gray and overcast), she remained outside on the landing for hours, indifferent to the cold and even to a freezing drizzle, which was getting heavier. About one in the afternoon she came back in and, "waking" me, said she needed to go do some work in the mountain town we had visited. It seemed she had to take some photos representing the region.

Soon on our way, we got there before dusk. The streets were deserted or, rather, filled with mounds of purple leaves, which moved in eddies from place to place. We stayed at the same hotel (or motel) as before; it was so quiet, we seemed to be its only guests. Before dark we went out into town, and she began to take some photos of houses still in the light. (If I appear in some of those photos, it's because she asked me to pose for her.) We went to the restaurant that reminded me of La Bodeguita del Medio. I noticed that Elisa had a ravenous appetite. Without losing her elegant composure, she downed several portions of soup, pasta, cream sauce, roast, bread, and dessert, besides two bottles of wine. Then she asked me to take her for a walk. The streets were narrow and badly lit, and after coming out of a place that so resembled La Bodeguita del Medio, it seemed as if I were back in Havana during my last years there. But what most brought me back to those days was a sensation of fear, of terror, even, which seemed to emanate from every corner and every object, including our own bodies. Night had fallen, and though there was no moon, there was a radiant luminosity in the sky. The usual evening fog enveloped everything, even ourselves, in a gray mist that blurred all silhouettes. Finally we reached a yellowish esplanade, which no car seemed to have crossed ever before. Elisa was walking ahead with all her equipment. The road narrowed and disappeared between dim promontories that looked like tapering, greenish rocks. Or like withered cypresses linked by a strange viscosity. On the other side of the promontories we came upon a lake, also greenish and covered by the same nebulous vegetation. Elisa deposited her expensive equipment on the ground and looked at me. As she talked, her face, her hair, and her hands seemed to glow.

"*Il veleno de la conoscenza é una della tante calamitá di cui soffre l'essere umano,*" she said, her eyes fixed on me. "*Il veleno della conoscenza o al meno quello della curiositá.*"*

*Poor Ramoncito wrote only the phonetic representation of these phrases. With my extensive knowledge of the Italian language (I studied with Giolio B. Blanc), I was able to make the necessary corrections. I must clarify that this is the only correction I have made in the manuscript. The translation into English would read like this: "The poison of knowledge is one of the many calamities humans suffer. The poison of knowledge, or, at least, that of curiosity." —D. S.

Even though his translation is correct, we doubt very much that Mr. Sakuntala ever studied with Baron Giolio B. Blanc. The high social status of this nobleman would not have permitted him to rub elbows with people like Mr. Sakuntala, let alone accept him as his tutee, unless there were highly personal motives. —Lorenzo and Echurre, 1999

Giolio B. Blanc was for many years the editor of the magazine Noticias de Arte de Nueva York and therefore had probably met Daniel Sakuntala, who had literary pretensions. —Editors, 2025

"I don't understand a word," I blurted out in all sincerity.

"Well, I want you to understand. I have never killed anybody without first telling him why."

"Who are you going to kill?" I asked her with a smile, to let her know I was not taking her words seriously.

"Listen to me, you fool," she said, stepping away from me while I, pretending not to understand, tried to embrace her. "I know everything you did. Your trips to the museum, your incessant surveillance, your detective work. Your pretended snoring did not fool me either. Of course, until now your stupidity and your cowardice have prevented you from seeing things as they are. Let me help you. There is no difference between what you saw in the painting at the museum and me. We are one and the same thing."

I must confess that it was impossible for me then to assimilate Elisa's words. I asked her to explain in simpler language, still hoping it was all a joke or the effect of the two bottles of wine.

After she repeated the same explanation several times, I finally got an idea of what she meant. The woman in the painting and Elisa were one and the same. As long as the painting existed, she, Elisa, would exist too. But for the picture to exist, she had, of course, to be there. That is, whenever the museum was open, she had to remain there inside the picture—"smiling, impassive, and radiant," as she put it, with a tinge of irony. Once the museum was closed, she could get out and have her amorous escapades like the ones I had participated in. "Encounters with men, the handsomest men I can find," she explained, looking at me, and in spite of my dangerous situation, I could not help but experience some feelings of vanity. . . . "But all those men," continued Elisa, "cannot simply *enjoy;* they want to *know,* and they end up like you, with a vague idea of my peculiar condition. Then the persecution begins. They want to know who I am, no matter what the cost; they want to know everything. And in the end, I have to eliminate them. . . ." Elisa paused for a moment and, glaring at me, continued: "Yes, I like men, and very much, because I am also a man, as well as a genius!" She said this looking at me, and I could see that her anger was mounting; realizing I was facing a dangerous madwoman, I decided it was best to "go with her flow" (as we used to say in Havana), and, begging her to control herself, I asked her to tell me about her sex change. "After all," I tried to console her, "New York is full of transvestites, and they don't look so unhappy. . . ." Completely ignoring my words, she explained to me: Not only was Elisa the woman in the painting, but the woman in the painting was also the painter, who had done his self-portrait as he wished to be (the way he was in his mind): a lusty, fascinating woman. But his real triumph was not that he portrayed himself as an alluring woman. "That," she said with scorn, "had already been done by most painters." His true achievement was that through a mustering of energy, genius, and mental concentration—which, she claimed, were unknown in our century—the woman he painted had the ability to become the painter himself and to outlive him. This person (she? he?) would then exist as long as the painting existed, and had the power, when nobody was present, to step out of the painting and escape into the crowds. And in this way she was able to find sexual gratification with the kind of men that the painter, as a man not graced by beauty, had never been able to get. *"But the power of concentration I must muster to achieve all that does not come easily. And now, after almost five hundred years, I some-*

57

times lose the perfection of my physical attributes or even one of my parts, as you on several occasions were astonished to see but could not believe."

In brief, I was facing a man over five hundred years old who had transformed himself into a woman and also existed as a painting. The situation would have been truly hilarious were it not for the fact that, at that point, Elisa drew from her bodice an ancient dagger, sharp and glimmering nonetheless.

I tried to disarm her, but in vain. With only one hand she overpowered me, and in an instant I was on the ground, the dagger before my eyes. Crouching, and imprisoned under Elisa's legs, I still was able to identify the landscape around us. It was exactly the same as in the famous (and now, for me, accursed) painting at the museum. Something sinister was indeed going on, though I could not determine its extent. Elisa—I will keep calling her Elisa until the end of this report—made me move along in my crouched position until we reached the lakeshore. Once there, I saw it was not a lake but a swamp. This was obviously the place, I thought, where she sacrificed her surely numerous indiscreet lovers.

The alternatives Elisa seemed to be offering me were equally frightful: to die either drowned in that swamp or pierced by the dagger. Or perhaps she had both in mind. Again she fixed her gaze on me, and I understood that my end was near. I started to cry. Elisa took off her clothes. I continued crying. It was not my family in Cuba that I remembered at that moment but the enormous salad bar at Wendy's. To me it was like a vision of my life these last few years (fresh, pleasant, surrounded by people, and problem-free), before Elisa came into it. Meanwhile she lay naked in the mud.

"Let it not be said," she muttered, barely moving her lips, "that we are not parting on the best of terms."

And beckoning me to join her, she kept smiling in her peculiar way, lips almost closed.

I couldn't stop crying, but I came closer. Still holding the dagger, she placed her hand behind my head, quickly aligning her naked body with mine. She did this with such speed, professionalism, and violence that I realized it would be very difficult for me to come out of that embrace alive. I am sure that in all my long erotic experience, never has my performance been so lustful and tender, so skillful and passionate, because in all truth, even knowing she intended to kill me, I still lusted for her. By her third orgasm, while she was still panting and uttering the most obscene words, Elisa had not only forgotten the dagger but become oblivious of herself. I noticed she apparently was losing the concentration and energy that, as she said, enabled her to become a real woman. Her eyes were becoming opaque, her face was losing its color, her cheekbones were melting away. Suddenly her luscious hair dropped from her head, and I found myself in the arms of a very old, bald man, toothless and foul-smelling, who kept whimpering while slobbering on my penis. Quickly he sat on it, riding it as if he were a true demon. I quickly put him on all fours and, in spite of my revulsion, tried to give him as much pleasure as I could, hoping he would be so exhausted he would let me go. Since I had never practiced sodomy, I wanted to keep the illusion, even remotely, that this horrible thing, this sack of bones with the ugliest of beards, was still Elisa. So while I possessed him, I kept calling him by that name. But he, in the middle of his paroxysm, turned and looked at me; his eyes were two empty reddish sockets.

"Call me Leonardo, damn it! Call me Leonardo!" he shouted, while writhing and groaning with such pleasure as I have never seen in a human being.

"Leonardo!" I began repeating, then, while I possessed him. "Leonardo!" I repeated as I kept penetrating that pestiferous mound. "Leonardo," I kept whispering tenderly, while with a quick jump I got hold of the dagger; then, flailing my arms, I escaped as fast as I could through the yellow esplanade. "Leonardo! Leonardo!" I was still shouting when I jumped onto my motorcycle and dashed away at full speed. "Leonardo! Leonardo! Leonardo!" I think I kept saying, still in a panic, all the way back to New York, as if repeating the name might serve as an incantation to appease that lecherous old man still writhing at the edge of the swamp he himself had painted.

I was sure that Leonardo, Elisa, or "that thing" was not dead.

Even more, I think I'd managed to do no harm at all to it. And if I did, would a single stab be enough to destroy all the horror that had managed to prevail for over five hundred years and included not only Elisa but the swamp, the sandy road, the rocks, the town, and even the ghostly mist that covered it all?

That night I slept in the home of my friend the Cuban writer Daniel Sakuntala.* I told him I had problems with a woman and did not want to sleep with her in my apartment.

*"Cuban writer Daniel Sakuntala" (!): We question this statement, obviously the product of friendship. Not even the lengthiest directories register that name.
—Lorenzo and Echurre, 1999

Without giving him any more details, I presented him with the dagger, which he was able to appreciate as the precious jewel it was. Would it solve any problem, I wondered, if I told him of my predicament? Would he believe me?* Right now, only two days away from my imminent demise, when there is no way out for me, I am telling my story mainly as an act of pure desperation and as my last hope, because nothing else is left for me to do. At least for now, I realize how very difficult it is for anyone to believe all this. Anyway, before the little time I have left runs out, let me continue.

Of course I did not, even remotely, consider going back to my room, terrified as I was by the possibility of finding Elisa there. I was sure of only one thing: she was looking for me, and still is, in order to kill me. This is what my own instinct, my experience of fear and persecution, are telling me (and don't forget I lived twenty years in Cuba).

For three days I roamed the streets without knowing what to do and, naturally, without being able to sleep. On Wednesday night I showed up again at Daniel's. I was shaking, not only out of fear but because I was running a fever. Maybe I had caught the flu, or something worse, during the time I was out on the streets.

Daniel behaved like a real friend, perhaps the only one I had and, I believe, still have. He prepared something for me to

*A serious error of appreciation on the part of my friend Ramoncito. After studying for more than twenty years and with the superior knowledge I acquired of alchemy, astrology, metempsychosis, and the occult sciences, I would have believed him and could have helped him to conjure away this evil. Had he trusted me, Ramoncito would be alive today. By the way, the dagger he gave me (pure gold, with an ivory handle) has disappeared from my room. I am sure it was taken by a black man from the Dominican Republic who accompanied Renecito Cifuentes when he visited me a few days ago. —D. S.

eat and hot tea, made me take two aspirins, and even gave me some syrupy potion.* Finally, after so many nights of insomnia, I fell asleep. I dreamed, of course, of Elisa. Her cold eyes were looking at me from a corner of the room. Suddenly that corner became the strange landscape with the promontories of greenish rocks around a swamp. By the swamp, Elisa was waiting for me. Her eyes were fixed on mine, her hands elegantly entwined below her chest. She kept looking at me with detached perversity, and her look was a command to get closer and embrace her right at the edge of the swamp. . . . I dragged myself there. She placed her hands on my head and pulled me down close to her. As I possessed her, I sensed that I was penetrating not even an old man but a mound of mud. The enormous and pestiferous mass slowly engulfed me while it kept expanding, splattering heavily and becoming more foul-smelling. I screamed as this viscous thing swallowed me, but my screams only produced a dull gurgling sound. I felt my skin and my bones being sucked away by the mass of mud, and once inside it, I became mud, finally sinking into the swamp.

My own screams woke me up so suddenly that I still had time to see Daniel sucking my member. He pretended it wasn't so and withdrew to the opposite side of the bed, making believe he was asleep, but I understood I could not stay there either. I got up, made some coffee, thanked Daniel for his hospitality and allowing me to sleep in his apartment, borrowed twenty dollars from him, and left.†

*The "syrupy potion" I gave him was just Riopan, a stomach relief medication against diarrhea. —D. S.
†Out of pure intellectual honesty, I am leaving this passage as it appears in the manuscript by my friend Ramoncito. I want the text to be published in its entirety. But the lascivious abuse he refers to can only be a product of his psycho-

Mona

It was Thursday. I had decided to leave New York before Monday. But with only twenty dollars, where could I go? I saw several acquaintances (Reinaldo García Remos, among them) and offered the key to my room, and everything in it, in exchange for some money. I got a lot of excuses but no cash. Late on Sunday I went to Wendy's, where, as a security guard, I had spent the best part of my life. At the cash register I talked to the stout black woman who had been so good to me (in every sense of the word). She let me have a salad, a quart of milk, and a hamburger, all for free. About five o'clock in the morning, the establishment was deserted and I dozed off on my seat. Another employee who was mopping the second floor called the cashier to pass on some piece of gossip. While they chatted, I took advantage of the situation and grabbed all the money from the cash register. Without counting it, I ran to Grand Central. I wanted to take a train and go as far as possible. But the three long-distance trains would not leave until nine in the morning. I sat on a bench and, while waiting, began to count the money. There was twelve hundred dollars. I thought this was salvation. By eight A.M. the station was swarming with people—or rather with beasts: thousands of people who pushed and shoved mercilessly to make it to work

---

logical state and of the nightmare he was having. It is true we slept that night on the same bed; it's the only one I have. I heard him scream, and to bring him out of his delirium, I shook him several times. Naturally, when he woke up, it was logical for him to find my hands on his body. —D. S.

We are of the opinion that Ramón Fernández was sexually harassed, as he indicates, by Mr. Sakuntala. The moral history of this character, who disappeared naked into Lake Erie in the midst of a communal orgy, proves our point. —Lorenzo and Echurre, 1999

We have already indicated that Daniel Sakuntala disappeared close to the shore of Lake Ontario, where his clothes were found. We have not been able to confirm reports about a supposed orgy. —Editors, 2025

on time. By nine, I hoped, I would be sitting on a train, fleeing from all those people and, above all, from that thing.

But it didn't turn out that way. I was standing in line to buy my ticket when I saw Elisa. She was below the big terminal clock, oblivious to the crowd but with her eyes fixed on me, with her enigmatic smile and her folded hands. I saw her coming my way and started to run toward the tracks. But since I did not have a ticket, I could not get in. Pushing people, and trying to find a place to hide, I went across the room again. But she was everywhere. I remember dashing through the Oyster Bar, colliding with a waiter, and upsetting a table on which a number of lobsters were arrayed. At the back door of the restaurant, Elisa was waiting for me. I knew, or sensed, that I could not stay alone with that "woman" a second longer, that the larger the crowd around me, the harder it would be for her to kill me or drag me into her swamp. I began screaming in English and in Spanish, begging for help, while I pointed at her. But the people, the masses of people, rushed by without looking at me. One more madman shouting in the most crowded train station in the world could not alarm anyone. Besides, my clothes were dirty and I had not shaved for a week. On the other hand, the woman I was accusing of attempted assault was a grand lady, serene, elegant, expertly made up and attired. I realized that I was not going to attract anybody's attention by shouting, so I rushed to the very center of the main hall, where it was most crowded, and quickly took off my clothes and stood there, naked. Then I began to jump about in the crowd. Evidently that was more than even a madman is allowed to do in the very center of the city of New York. I heard some police whistles.

Arrested, I felt relieved and peaceful, for the first time in many days, as they handcuffed me and shoved me roughly into the patrol car.

Unfortunately, I only stayed overnight at the police station. There was no evidence on which to hold me as a criminal of any sort, and if I was insane—and I quote the officer in charge—"luckily, that would not be a matter for the New York police; otherwise, we would have to arrest almost everybody." As for the money, it had disappeared into the hands of the arresting officers when they searched my clothes. So there was no evidence that I had committed any crime. Of course, among other things, I confessed to being a thief, which was nothing but the truth, and mentioned the money that had been stolen from me. Apparently the police found no computer record of any accusation by the Wendy's management or any report of the loss of that money.*

On Tuesday I was again roaming the streets of Manhattan. The drizzle and strong winds were unbearable, and I had no money at all and no umbrella either, of course. It was eleven A.M. I knew the Metropolitan Museum would be open until seven that evening, so for the moment, at least, I was in no danger. Inside the picture frame, she would now be smiling at all her admirers. It was then (I recall I was crossing 42nd Street) that I had a sort of epiphany. An idea that could really save me. Why hadn't I thought of it before? I brained

---

*It seems that Ramoncito Fernández had, without being aware of it, a woman who really loved him: the Wendy's cashier. From my investigation I learned that out of her salary she had, little by little, covered the so-called embezzlement that occurred while she was in charge, without ever disclosing the name of the thief. Obviously that woman was another person, besides me, whom Ramoncito could have asked for help, had he been more trusting and less obstinate. —D. S.

myself for being such a fool, particularly when I pride myself on not being a complete idiot. The painting! The painting, of course! There she was, and the swamp, the rocks, the yellow esplanade. . . . Everything the painter had conceived, including even himself, was now in the museum, fulfilling its destiny as a work of art and at the mercy of whomever dared to destroy it.

Back in my room, I took a hammer I use for my occasional carpentry,* and hiding it under my jacket, I rushed to the Metropolitan Museum. There I met with another little inconvenience: I had no money to pay for admission. Of course I could force my way in, but I didn't want to be arrested before doing my work. Finally someone coming out of the building agreed to give me the metal badge that indicates you have paid for admission. I clipped it onto my jacket and entered the building. Running to the second floor, I went into the most visited gallery in the museum. There she was, captive inside the frame, smiling at her audience. Pushing the stupid crowd away, I rushed in, brandishing my hammer. I was finally going to do away with the monstrosity that had destroyed so many men and that very soon would destroy me too. But then, just as I was ready to hit the first blow, one of Elisa's hands moved away from the other, and with incredible speed (while her expression remained impassive), she pressed the alarm button on the wall next to her painting. Suddenly a steel curtain dropped from the ceiling, covering the painting completely.†

---

*It is true that Ramoncito knew about carpentry. He built me an excellent bookcase once. The hammer in question was not his but mine. I had lent it to him when he installed the air-conditioning in his studio with the help of Miguel Correa. —D. S.

†This protection system is the most efficient ever devised. At the same time the alarm goes off, the metal curtain drops over the wall where the piece of art is

And, hammer in hand, I was restrained by the museum security guards, by the police (who materialized instantly), and by the fanatic crowd that had come to worship that painting. The same crowd that in Grand Central had done nothing for me when I screamed for help because my life was in danger was the one that now shoved me angrily into the patrol car.

Today, Friday, after being under arrest for four days, I am coming to the end of my story, which I will try to send to Daniel as soon as possible. I may be able to do it. Quite unexpectedly, I have become a notorious character. There are two police officers here who seem to admire me because I am a strange case they cannot figure out. It was my intention not to steal a painting worth millions of dollars but to destroy it. One of the officers (I am withholding his name) has promised to get this manuscript out and give it to my friend Daniel. If this testimony reaches his hands soon enough, I do not know what he will be able to do, but I am sure he will do something. Maybe

---

being exhibited. It is very expensive to install. There are only three masterpieces in the world that have this protection. According to the research carried out by my friend Kokó Salás, the curator, the three works are: La Joconde, *by Leonardo da Vinci;* Guernica, *by Pablo Picasso; and* The Burial of Count Orgaz, *by Doménikos Theotokópoulos, El Greco.* —D. S.

*Daniel Sakuntala is completely misguided when he calls Kokó Salás a "curator." In all truth, he is a common criminal,** dedicated to the illegal traffic of works of art in Madrid, under the protection of the Cuban government in Havana.* —Lorenzo and Echurre, 1999

**To label Kokó Salás as a common criminal is to underestimate his character and historic significance. Kokó Salás was a sophisticated, gifted person (it is now impossible to determine whether he was a man or a woman) who worked for an international spy ring in service to the Kremlin. Under the secretary for mineral rights, Victorio Garrati, he conspired indefatigably and took part in intrigues until he finally achieved the annexation of Italy and Greece to the Soviet Union in the year 2011. For more information, see* La Matahari [sic] de Holguín, *by Teodoro Tapia.* —Editors, 2025

some influential person will read it; maybe it will be taken seriously and I will be granted personal protection, efficient full-time vigilance. Understand this: the fact is I don't want to get out of this prison cell; what I need is for Elisa not to get in. The ideal situation would be to install here the same metal curtain that protects her. But all that would have to be done before Monday. The museum closes that day, and she will be totally free and with time to accumulate all the energy and develop all the stratagems she needs in order to get to me here, to destroy me. Please, help me! Or else I will soon become another of her countless victims, those buried under that greenish swamp that you can see in the background of her famous painting, from which she is still watching, with those eyes without lashes, while she keeps smiling.

Miami Beach, October 1986

The Parade Begins

BEHIND—but pretty close to me—comes Rigo whistling, boots creaking. The Pupo sisters follow, holding hands with the boys, chatting, cackling, roaring with laughter, and calling Rigo to tell him I have no idea what. And behind them, the Estradas, and Rafael Rodríguez, Bartolo Angulo's children and Panchita's, and Cross-eyed Wilfredo. Behind them, Cándido Parronda's grandsons. Farther behind, the children of Tano's woman, Caridad. And Arturo, Old Rosa's son. And the people coming from La Loma, Perrera, and Guayacán. Up ahead, the women in the oxcarts, all fat-bellied, and a group of rebels; and the boys from the neighborhood. Even farther back, those on horses. And some bicycles, and then a truck. And Nino Ochoa on crutches. Then there is another truck that catches up with us as we come to El Majagual. And we have to press together on one side of the road to let it by. It's overflowing with people waving hats and raising a flag. Quite a stir. And the dust of the road is rising up, covering us and coming down, like trailing smoke, then up again because the horses' hooves are getting close, are next to us, are rushing ahead, forming a cloud that wraps us all around and I can barely see you. Even farther behind are a lot of people I don't know who seem to be singing. Maybe they have a radio. I can't tell. They are very far away. Maybe they are just talking, and from here it sounds like they are singing. Because everything seems to be singing. And when I hear Rigo's voice—he's catching up with me again, is already next to me—saying "I stink like a bear's nuts," even that has a ring to it. "And me too," I say, "me too." And we are now walking together. And we become part of the great parade that grows bigger and bigger. I lose sight of him in the crowd, but he waits for me. And he's again walking by my side. And talking about smells. "I'm dying for a shower," he tells me. "What a nice shower I'll have as soon as I get home." And I look at him again, laughing. I look at you. I see you in your ragged military uniform, walking by my side, mingling with the massive crowd and the horses, a real mob. You, wearing this impressive uniform, now so tattered you have trouble keeping your body covered; and the rifle on your shoulder, held together with wires. And the people coming up to you. And the Pupo sisters trying to start a conversation. They talk to you, only to you. Not to me, not at all, no way. I'm carrying nothing. I didn't want to. I couldn't. . . . I was at the brook, filling cans with water to be stored in my aunt Olga's earthenware jars. I was there when I heard the shots. The shooting is starting again, I thought. But then I heard laughter, and loud shouts of *"Viva Cuba libre"* (it's amazing, they're using that old war cry), and I started to run, leaving the cans where the current would surely drag them away, and without saying good-bye to my aunt. I was still panting when I got to the main road. The Pupo sisters were already at their gate. They, and the other people joining in, told me the news, so unexpected I couldn't believe it. When I was at the brook filling the cans with water (already on my second trip), I was thinking, My God, there is no end to this; these people will never win the war with such dilapidated weapons. I will have to stay here forever, hiding, fleeing; I'll never be able to return to Holguín. Sleeping with the rats and vegetables in the storage shed. With no other hope than a remote claim from an uncle in the States, who has been washing dishes forever, and still writes to us. *The oxcarts, and the goad-sticks sinking in the oxen's backs: "Giddyap, you bastards." The horses' hooves make the dust cloud rise, come up to us, fall on us suddenly and enclose us like in a mosquito net. Until you appear again, your uniform torn, your rifle swaying. After failing to settle it on your shoulder, you finally brandish it triumphantly.* "Here, take a shot," you told me. I took the rifle and pulled it to my chest in order to take aim. "Not that way," you said. I returned the rifle to you and didn't try again. And then I waited; for more than a month I waited there in the camp. Among the rebels, doing nothing, listening to their dirty jokes, shooing the gnats away. Having a shot of rum once in a while. Eating charred meat from the cows given to us by the people or (according to them) bought by us on credit. Then I was told: Those who come without rifles can no longer join the rebels. And together with that piece of news, forty-eight men and seven women came down from the Sierra after being rejected; there is no room for any more unarmed volunteers. Every day there are more without even a pistol who want to join. "Rifles!" "Rifles!" "Without rifles we can't take you in." And let's face it, what good is an unarmed army? I have to go back. But it's too late. I left a note on the bed. I said, "Dear Mom, I'm leaving to join the rebels because here I'm doing nothing." That's what I said, and then added, "Don't say a word to anyone." And I signed it. *And now after crossing the Majagual River, the caravan is getting bigger, it's wider and longer; and the people from Las Carreteras, and also those from Perronales and Guajabales, are getting closer to us. They are all coming from behind, catching up with us, and are getting ahead already. They shout as they walk: they are almost running now. The dust cloud swallows them. And you, in your uniform, sweating, but so proud, lifting your rifle. Talking about your body odors. "Me too," I say. Then I keep silent. And I look at my hands, full of calluses from carrying all those water cans. And then, almost with shame, I look at my civilian clothes. And we keep walking. You, totally unaware, keep chatting. "And my mom, and my chick, everybody's waiting for me," you say. The ruckus becomes deafening at times. A bottle of Paticruzado is being passed around. We take a sip. And now we're red in the face because of the rum and the heat, wrapped in that dust cloud that settles and rises, that dances in front of us and then goes up, covering our faces, erasing us for a few moments; we keep moving ahead. I was right: the people behind us were singing; they are singing, someone has a guitar. When we get to the Lirio River, the laughter, the singing, and the clip-clop of the horses is tremendous. I can barely hear you. And you are shouting. "What?" I shout back. "How things went for you, where did you end up after Velasco?" And we continue the march, covered with sweat. You, with your uniform so wet that it sticks to your butt. Still enveloped by the dust cloud that keeps com-*

ing up. In half an hour or less we'll be in Holguín. I don't answer you; but the knife you gave me is here, under my shirt. I touch it, embarrassed, but don't show it to you. Side by side, we are both practically running. Trying to avoid the horses, we jump to the other side of the road. You keep talking. "Yeah," I say. "Yeah." Though with all the commotion I practically can't hear you now. Suddenly I hear nothing. Nothing. I hear nothing, though I know the uproar is incredible. Someone is looking at me, someone else stumbles into me and goes on. Maybe the women are shouting, maybe they're crying with joy. I don't know, because I don't hear anything anymore. There is nothing but silence. But I do see; I see you going into the river. You're not crossing it over the rocks. Your creaking boots plunge into the muddy water. I am still behind, almost next to you, my shoes also sink in. We find the water refreshing. Maybe we don't feel the heat so much now. But as usual, my hands are perspiring. Because everything is unbearable; because for the past few months we haven't had electricity; the school was closed and the roads into town were blockaded by the rebels, there was nothing to eat, not even a drop of milk. "Ave Maria," Grandma says, "we're going to starve to death." And me, in the living room, now unable to listen to Miguel Aceves Mejía. And me in the living room, in the rocking chair, not knowing what to do. And Grandpa spraying the mosquitoes night after night; with nothing to eat and the house full of mosquitoes, cockroaches, and mice. Mice! Any day now they will come sniffing up to my bed, and pull me by the feet, and carry me I don't know where, into their dark caves, there where the world ends. For all that, and because I was sick of this damned town that has never seen and will never ever see the ocean. And because one almost can't go out, either by day or night. And I only have the living room left (this furnace) since the kitchen and the dining room are Grandma, Grandpa, and Mother's space. And to top it all, I don't have a penny to my name because the factory closed some time ago. So here I am, not knowing what to do, just listening to the shooting. Every evening, every single evening, I listen to the shooting. "The rebels are already in Bayamo." "They are already in Cacocún." "They took La Chomba." "Last night they entered Loma de la Cruz." Very soon they will take this town, and me here in this rocking chair, confined, just hearing the wheezing of the insect sprayer that the old man brandishes with amazing dexterity. And the old woman moaning: "Oh, dear, we're going to starve to death." And the old man: "Idiots, they think they can win a war with just flags." And my mother: "What a cruel fate, what a cruel fate." And Lourdes: "Do you love me or don't you? Tell me, once and for all." And all the cockroaches, and the immortal mosquitoes. Because of all that, and this stifling heat (the house has a fiber-cement roof), and because of this hot town, stuck in the midland, without sidewalks or shaded arcades, with so very few trees. For all that, and heaven knows for how many other things. And without a quarter to buy rum. Not even a nickel, which could buy the cheapest shot. And not being able to have homemade tamarind wine (because in this town we aren't getting tamarind either). I know the rebels are closing in. I know that at the front over the hill they put up a sign that reads: "Only real men have gotten this far." I know that people say the rebels sent a box full of panties to the base in Holguín. But that is not for me. I can't stand this horrendous place anymore. I . . . *We are starting the third crossing of the river. The horses are rearing in the water. One of them goes into the current. Many of the women scream. We keep on marching. You are ahead, and turn around to look at me. You are getting all the praise, all the glances from the Pupo sisters. You adjust the rifle on your shoulder and go right on talking. We are both soaked.* And so that evening after dinner I went to see Tico. "Hey," I told him, "we're not doing anything here. Why don't we join?" He was half-asleep on the sofa. His parents were in the living room. "I'll come for you very early in the morning," I told him. "We can walk to Velasco. The rebels are there. We tell them that we want to join, and that's it." "Okay," he says, still lying on the sofa. "See you tomorrow," I say. *There is more shooting now, loud noise, laughter and singing. Very soon we'll be in town.* In the evening, the old man sprays more insecticide. I don't know which is more horrendous: the fury of the mosquitoes or the smell of petroleum. I can't decide. But early tomorrow morning I'll be very far away. I'm leaving. At the crack of dawn, I get up and dress without making any noise. (Luckily, my grandparents didn't do anything last night; other times they don't let me sleep a wink with their loud noises.) "Dear Mother," I write on a piece of paper. I'm leaving, cautiously opening the door. I'm already in the street. *The trotting of the horses, the bustle of the crowds; the laughter. And over there the oxcarts. Now the bicycles are going by, brushing against me, stirring the dust that comes up in our faces. "Let's climb on a cart," you say. But we don't even try. All sweaty, we keep walking with the noisy throng. A truck blows its horn. "Coming through," the driver shouts. The truck makes its way through the crowd; people jump to the side of the road. "Coming through, coming through," the driver keeps shouting.* "Tico," I said not very loudly. "Tico," I said again. But he did not answer. He was asleep, or maybe he was just pretending. I took the road to Gibara; I walked along the edge of the road without trying to hitch a ride. I go alone up to Aguasclaras. There I join a group of women with newborn babies who are on their way to Velasco. "My father lives there," I tell them. I give them a name. I help them with their children. We are passing by the dam when some young government soldiers call out to us. Now I'm in trouble; but no. "It's the same people from last week," the *casquitos* say, and they let us go on. After a hike of twenty miles, we're in Velasco. *Voices, incredibly loud voices. Another bottle of Pati-cruzado. "You drink first," you tell me. "No, you," I say; but I do drink. We are red again. It's too hot, too dusty. We feel sticky. We continue forging ahead, close to each other. He keeps talking to me.* But there are no rebels in this town. And I've already eaten, as soon as I arrived, the forty-five cents' worth of pound cake I had brought with me. I sit down in the park, under a tree. I'm waiting, but there is no rebel in sight. There is only a man sitting on the opposite bench, watching me. He's been watching me for a while. Maybe he's been assigned to watch me. He stands up; he's coming over. Perhaps he's going to take me to the police headquarters, where they'll torture me, gouge my eyes out. . . . "Hey, boy, where are you from?" he asks. "From Holguín." And we fall silent, both of us still looking at each other. "You have relatives here?" "No." Again we are silent. He's still watching me. But then, after we've stared at each other for an eternity, it's maybe past midday, he talks to me in a low, deep voice. "Boy," he says, "you are here to join the rebels, aren't you?" "Yes," I say, thinking that now there is no escape, that it's already . . . "Of seven brothers," he says, "I'm the only one who hasn't joined. Though I'm also a little bristled." And he takes me first to his mother's, and later to the camp. "Look at what those rebels did to me when they passed through town," the mother says while she takes me around the house. "The bastards, they even smashed my lard jars." After dark, the man leads me to the rebel headquarters in Sierra de Gibara. And that is where I meet you, at the gate. On guard duty with your dilapidated rifle. "Halt!" you say. The man greets you and gives you the password. "I'm bringing this boy who wants to join," he says, pointing at me. You glance at me; then you light a cigarette and offer me one. *Behind the carts crammed with big-bellied women, the thunder of horses' hooves; behind the horses, the honking trucks, then the bicycles, and after, thousands of people on foot. And above everything, the great dust cloud that rises and comes down, settles and comes up again as if exploding, enveloping us. Ahead and behind us, up above and below, everywhere, is this huge cloud of dust raised by the caval-cade.* And I kept you company when you were at your post, though you never lent me your rifle again. We did the same guard duty, and we talked. Like this. Day after day. After day. "Look at this photo," you said. "It's my mother, poor thing." "Look at this photo," you said. "It's my girlfriend; I'm really going to get her good as soon as I get out. I've been here eleven months, just think what a dry spell!" *Ahead and above, below and behind, the great dust cloud. And now this singing. An anthem. You're singing too. And I pretend to be singing, though I'm not. We keep sweating a lot.* I'd been there just over a month when forty-eight men and seven women came down from the Sierra. All covered with mud, exhausted after the long walk. You and I bring them water in canteens. Then we all wait for the arrival of the captain. And for his speech. "My dear peo-ple," he says, "we cannot admit any more rebel soldiers who come with nothing except goodwill. We need rifles. Without rifles we cannot accept anybody." Rifles! Rifles! You leave your post for a moment and we walk down to the coconut grove, where there is some shade. We crouch. We pick some mallows and begin to eat them. We stay there for a while. But not long, because I can't stay in the camp and you have to return to your post. "I'm leaving," I say. When we are both standing you reach under your shirt. "Take this," you tell me, and hand me a knife, sheath and all. "Go to Holguín and knock off a novice soldier. Get his rifle, and come back here." I don't say anything to you. I don't thank you. It's late. I come down from the Sierra and get back to Velasco. At dusk I leave for Holguín. "You dig it in," you said. *From out of the dust comes the sound of a transistor radio above the ruckus. The voice from the radio, the anthems. The big news. The dictator fled: it has been confirmed. There is a list of those who escaped. A list of those arrested. Shouts of "Viva." Great uproar. The Pupo sisters burst out laughing. A horse rears, threatening to kick some women, who move aside, screaming. And we are already in Atejón. In five minutes we'll be in Holguín.* I wait until midnight before going into town. I knock on the door. "Who is it?" Grandpa whispers behind the closed jalousies. "It's me," I say. "It's me." He opens the door very cautiously. "Boy," he says. Behind him, my mother, wrapped in a bedsheet; and Grandma. Both are screaming; both cry as they embrace me. The sheet slips, Mother is almost naked. "Hush," Grandpa whispers. "Hush, we're going to wake up the neighbors." "Oh, my boy," Mother says, and keeps hugging me. I manage finally to get untangled and push her away. And on my feet, in the middle of the living room, I start talking. "I just came back to kill a casquito, get his rifle, and go back to the Sierra." And I take out the knife. Then, for the first time, I draw it from its sheath and look at it, dazzled. Its brand-new blade glimmers. It has a horn handle and a daunting edge like a switchblade. My mother screams, and shrinks back in the rocking chair. "You're crazy," Grandma says. "You

think you're already a man at fourteen. Enough nonsense. Get to bed." Grandpa comes up mumbling, trying to take the knife away. But I jump quickly and evade him. I reach the front door and run out. "Don't shout," I hear Grandpa saying. "They are going to burn the house on account of that fool."
The caravan of bicycles goes by, pushing us aside again, lifting the dry, dusty soil; some have flat tires and are being carried on shoulders or dumped on the oxcarts loaded with women and young men. One of the Pupo women is calling out for her son, who got lost. We hear the strumming of a guitar; the singing continues. The parade is spectacular. The third bottle of Paticruzado reaches us. Sweaty, we keep marching close together. Your moist arm touches mine, already soaked. A casquito is on guard duty, standing in front of the electric plant. He moves once in a while. He walks from one side of the metal entry gate to the other, shouldering his rifle. He whistles. He goes to and fro. He stands still. Then the casquito looks around, and, slowly, I keep moving closer. At times I furtively reach back to feel the knife still there, under my shirt. The casquito is wearing very shiny boots; he's strong and slender under his tight khaki pants. He seems to be a very light mulatto, though I cannot see him very well in the darkness. I keep getting closer. The casquito is very young. I cross in front of him, stop at the other corner, and look back. I think he's also looking at me. I continue walking. I stop. I go back. Now, a bit closer, I stop again and look at him. He also looks at me. We have been eyeing each other for a while. Now he walks by the large gate from one side to the other and faces me. He teases me. Perhaps he thinks I'm gay, and that I am just leading him on. He takes a few steps toward me. He whistles. Goes back. He faces me and again scratches himself. He keeps whistling. I remain on the corner, looking at him for a while.

Finally, I start walking home. I knock on the door. Now it's way past midnight. Nobody asks who it is. The door opens, and there again is my mother, wrapped in the bedsheet. She hangs around my neck. "Oh, my son," she says, "you're crazy. Give me that knife. Don't you see you are the only thing I have." Still crying, she puts her arms around me. In the hallway I see my grandparents, motionless. They look alike. My mother keeps talking to me, and I think how ridiculous her words sound. And seeing her like that, embracing me, all teary-eyed and saying so many silly things, I feel like punching her. But I don't. And even though I don't know why, I begin crying too. *Throngs of people, and then the frightened dogs, barking, rolling in the dust, and yelping when people thoughtlessly kick them. And the creaking of the oxcarts, the clip-clop of the horses, the drone of the trucks. The bicycles disappear on the dusty road. And you by my side, still shouldering your rifle, your uniform soaked and covered with dust. You talk. And talk. And talk. A woman comes up to you and gives you a salacious smile. You keep talking and I try to listen to you. Once in a while I catch myself feeling for the knife under my shirt. We are entering the town already. "You damn son of a bitch," shouts one of the Pupo girls when someone pinches her bottom.* I spend a day under the bed, hiding. "Don't make him any fried eggs," Grandpa says. "The noise might give us away." In the evening Uncle Benedicto parks his car in front of the house. My mother quickly throws a towel over my shoulders. Grandma traps me under an old hat. Mother and I climb in the car, which starts moving without the lights turned on. The car takes us to Atejón. "It's dangerous to continue in the car," Benedicto says. "Either the casquitos or the rebels could stop us, even take the car away." And now the boring peregrination with my mother. We go to

Arcadio's, to Guilo's. Anywhere we know someone. One day here and another day somewhere else. Anyplace where we can get some food. Until finally, after a lot of my mother's pleading (I never once opened my mouth to ask for anything), I manage to get to my aunt Olga's. And I stay (while Mother goes back to town), and carry water and firewood for Aunt Olga, working all day long to pay for my bed and board while hiding from the police. At times, when I'm taking the empty water cans to the brook, I begin to sing. And one day I spent some time fishing for *pitises*. And once, night was catching up with me while I was still at the brook. I then took out the knife you gave me, which I always carry beneath my shirt, and started looking at it. I slid my finger along the edge—was it ever sharp. And I stayed for quite a long time there, handling it, and whistling, not very loudly, under the *cupeyes* by the brook. I got back very late. My aunt was impatient. That day only half of the water cans were filled. But the following day I filled them up. And the next. And the next. And the one following. Always like that: filling those water cans. Here on this good-for-nothing hill, where you can't see any rebels and you can only hear the distant shooting. And I wonder how's your life in the Sierra. And I keep carrying water. Going to and coming from the brook; sometimes I bathe in the water hole; and sometimes I try catching pitises just for fun; sometimes I whistle a lot. And sometimes I think it would be best to . . . And here in the water, with my pants rolled up, I am just doing some thinking when I hear shots. Nearby shots. And then the rumble of crowds of people approaching and the shouts of "Viva!" And I drop the water cans, and start running down the savanna toward the main road. "Batista fled!" I hear at the gate of the Pupo sisters' farm, and the crowds start to come. And there, my clothes in tatters, I run with the crowd on the way to town. Right behind me are the people from Guayacán. The bicycles appear. An oxcart crammed with women is coming down the hill very slowly, following us. We're going past Cuatro Caminos, and that's where we meet our first group of rebels. They are coming from Velasco on foot, shooting in the air, shouting, *"Viva Cuba, cojones,"* and lots of other things. You are with them. I call out to you at the top of my lungs. As soon as you see me, you abandon your group and come running. You throw your arm around my shoulders, and begin talking. *Flags and more flags. Front and rear. High and low; in the arcades that suddenly spring up in the streets; on the telegraph poles at the first wide avenue; hanging from the laurel trees; on the doors and windows of every home. Scattered on the ground. Tied to a long series of ropes, and flapping in the wind. Flags. Thousands and thousands of flags, hastily set on remote corners. Red rags and black rags. Colored papers. Papers, papers. Rags. Because we are already entering Holguín. And all of us below the flags. And everybody is hollering. Shouting vivas. Singing. And ahead of us, tied to mops and broomsticks or any kind of pole, flags fluttering. And cars blowing their horns nonstop. And all the boys from the hill on one side of the road, watching us pass by. "There go the rebels," someone shouts. "There go the rebels." And now everybody flocks to you. And the whores from La Chomba and Pueblo Nuevo approach you. And one of them touches your face. "But look how young he is," she says. "He doesn't even have a beard." And you look at her and burst out laughing. Flags. Flags.* And suddenly there is loud noise, louder than before, and shouts of "To the execution wall! To the execution wall!" The people are shouting, "They caught a Mansferrer Tiger!" and they all run toward the center of the commotion. The rebels try to prevent the lynching of the henchman, and run to protect him with their rifles. An old woman goes up and manages to hit him. The crowd roars. They ask for his death. The henchman says nothing. He simply stares ahead. He seems to be in a distant world. And we continue advancing along the avenue full of flags. Until, ahead of us in the middle of the street, a tall, thin woman appears, all dressed in black. She's the mother of one of the henchman's victims. The woman stops the group. "Please, I beg of you," she says, "don't kill him, don't kill him. Punish him, but don't kill him!" Shedding profuse tears, she keeps pleading. But all of you, and all of us, start walking. The woman is being left behind, in the middle of the street full of flags. We get to a children's playground. Someone has fixed the town's power lines, and the lampposts light up. All the radios are blaring now with the latest anthems, which I had not yet heard. A group of rebels take the henchman to their headquarters. You stay in the park, surrounded by people. The women from La Chomba offer you cigarettes. They take you to a bench and begin asking you questions. You talk, always smiling, always showing off your rifle, but you don't allow anyone to touch it. I keep watching you. The crowd around you is growing by the minute, asking you questions, offering you praise. I raise my hand. I try to say good-bye, to tell you, "I'll see you around." But I can't get close enough. You are surrounded. It seems they are about to carry you on their shoulders. Now the military marches are louder. Near me, someone is mocking them at the top of his voice. "Viva, viva," some raggedy boys shout from the top of the fountain with the turtles. I am making my way on one side of the park, where the crowd is thinner. It is night already. I hear the first rockets. Suddenly the sky explodes in fireworks. I turn on Diez de Octubre Street and reach my neighborhood. Everybody is very excited; some of my neighbors greet me enthusiastically. I rush to get home. My mother and my grandparents are on the porch, waiting for me. The three of them embrace me at the same time. "Son," they all say. I go in. "You must be starving," Grandma says. "Can I fix you something?" "No," I say. And I sit in the dining room. Right then, Tico and Lourdes come in. "Hey, big man," Tico tells me. I shake his hand and hug Lourdes. Over the radio, which Mother has just turned on, a woman recites a patriotic poem. The anthems keep resounding in the streets. And now Grandpa comes in from his produce stand, carrying a red-and-black flag with a big number 26 in the middle. "Say, young man!" he says, and hands me the flag. "Go out in the street with it," Mother tells me. "All the neighbors are waiting for you." I stand there for a moment, holding the flag. "I'm tired," I finally say, and throw the flag into the bathroom. And I turn on the light. I take out the knife under my shirt and put it on the edge of the john. Before undressing, I take a look at my miserable civilian clothes, sweaty and muddy. Over the radio, the woman keeps reciting in a thundering voice. The marches reverberate in the street along with the rejoicing from all over town. "Hurry," my mother says outside the door. "We are waiting for you." I don't answer. Naked, I go under the shower and open the faucet. The water falls over my head, slides down my body, and is completely reddened with dust when it reaches the floor.

1965

In the Shade
of the Almond Tree

"WE'VE GOT TO CHOP IT DOWN," one of them says. And I rush out to the street. The other two burst out laughing, let out a snort of relief, and applaud. "We've got to chop it down," they echo in a circle around the first one. Finally they leave the dining room and head toward the patio. But I'm already on the street. It's cool. The brutal September sun is gone, and autumn settles in the trees. It feels almost pleasant to stroll on these streets. From here I don't see their prancing about, their intolerable shouting, their constant running back and forth through the house, unsettling everything, questioning everything, wearing down the patio tiles. They never stop even for a second, and when they got it into their heads to chop down the trees (complaining that too many fallen leaves kept them sweeping forever), they took to it with such eagerness that in a week all of them had been cut down. Only the almond tree, the one at the back of the patio, was still standing. Without realizing it, I'm walking into the heart of the old section in Havana. I cut across to Obispo Street, and, even though I'm not interested, I glance at the store windows, and stop for a moment by a few, looking without seeing, or reading absentmindedly even the titles of scientific books. I stand there looking at these unappetizing volumes for a while, until I realize that someone else is also looking at them, apparently with great interest. A gorgeous girl. I look at her from head to toe, and feel the urge to touch her. She takes a large comb out of her purse, fixes her hair, looks at me, and starts to walk, swaying her hips a bit. Her dress, short and tight, moves in rhythm with her body. Yes, I'm sure that she looked at me and that she even gave me a brief signal. Or I imagined it. . . . Anyway, I'm going to follow her. Next I find myself by the only almond tree still standing. I lie down on my back, and stay there in its shade all day, half-asleep. I feel the moist leaves falling on my face. But now this tree is also in danger. Its leaves sometimes land in the hallway, or worse, they end up in the living room. A few days ago a leaf circled down like a dying bird right onto the lap of one of my aunts, who apparently was mending a pair of pants in a rush. "This is the last straw!" she cried, throwing the pants on the floor and grabbing the leaf with such fury that it crumbled in her hands. Now she's walking ahead very slowly, maybe giving me time to catch up. I follow her closely down Obispo Street until we come to La Moderna Poesía. She stops briefly and then goes in. And now I'm really sure that she looked at me. She glances at the shelves, leafs through a few books, skims some of the pages. This is the moment to speak to her, before she gets bored and leaves, and since the almond tree is now the only one standing, all the birds in the neighborhood seek shelter in it. At dusk the din of the cackling birds reaches up to the house. My mother covers her ears with her hands and looks out angrily at the patio. All the birds have now settled in the tree. Cautiously I get closer, careful not to frighten them. I finally reach the tree trunk. Lying on my back, I listen to them screeching until it gets dark. Now she comes out of the bookstore, walking fast. Maybe she's offended because I didn't speak to her. Next she goes in the Manzana de Gómez shopping arcade and stops in front of a store window; then she crosses Central Park, and gets lost in the crowd. I speed up because I don't want to lose sight of her. I remain very still, listening to the uproar of the birds. The leaves are falling constantly and I try to collect them, to catch them up in the air before they clutter the ground. But there are too many. We are in October and the leaves fall. And fall. And fall. And no matter how much I leap about and hurry to catch them in flight, one always escapes, slips in through the window, and, skipping over the chairs, rolls softly and lands at the feet of one of my aunts. It's impossible to catch all the autumn leaves, and following her through this crowd of people is getting more and more difficult. It seems as if all of Havana has gathered on San Rafael Street. The endless lines, the bustle of people darting here and there, the cars and buses that spare no effort to run me down. But I manage to cut through the crowd. I race after the blue patch of her skirt. Suddenly I lose sight of her. I look all around for her. She's gone. And undoubtedly there is no spot in the world more pleasant than here: in the shade and close to the trunk, which remains moist as if it were constantly shedding its skin. Many new shoots are beginning to sprout.

The new leaves are a tender green. Sometimes I'm tempted to eat them. And I do. Surprisingly, I discover her again in front of the Duplex. I almost bump into her. She looks at me. I'm bathed in perspiration. She starts walking and I follow her closely. And this is how we get to the Five and Ten. For half an hour we stand in line waiting for a seat. We finally sit and, as she crosses her legs, her skirt rides up above her knees. She asks for a malted soda. I ask for the same, and pay for both. Now she's truly looking at me. I'm all excited. It's so difficult for me to get up again. When I am there, dozing in the shade, I always dream about the same thing more or less, the same dream, the same dog. Because it's a dog I'm dreaming about. I'm in an enormous house, full of people talking and talking (I don't know who these people are because I can hardly see their faces, and I can't make out what they're saying either), and when I'm about to leave, the dog appears at the door. It looks at me with its shiny eyes. Without barking, it comes up to me and sinks its teeth into my ankle. I go inside the house again. The people are still talking and talking. With my hands in my pockets, I try to leave as casually as possible, without looking down. She walks ahead of me and seems aware of my situation and rather amused by it. And this is how we reach the sidewalk. And sensing that there was little time left, I spoke to my mother on one of those days when she was almost calm and not even smoking. "At least we still have the almond tree," I said, "or else we'd be suffocating." She looked at me absently and then said, "If we let it be, one day we'll all indeed be smothered, buried under a pile of leaves." I say nothing and walk out to the patio. There, my three aunts, brooms in hand, are sweeping fanatically. For a moment I stop to look at them: they are all of the same height, tall and skinny, and have a frightened air as if anxiously expecting someone to come from behind and hit them. The three are sweeping together, making the same motions. The tree seems ablaze in its resplendent gold. A bird hidden in the branches is singing its heart out. And now it's raining. People crowd the arcades. She is on a corner, apparently looking at the street. It's not a violent downpour, just one of those endless showers. The trees in Fe del Valle Park glisten through the drizzle. Finally she starts walking toward the bus stop. A bus goes by, so crowded its door won't open. Another one comes; she takes it. I get on just as the door closes. But the conspiracy continues and there is nothing I can do. I thought about it over and over again but couldn't find a way to come to the rescue. Sometimes I felt like screaming or setting the house on fire. Finally I decided to speak to my father. "Papa," I said to him, "they want to chop down the only almond tree we have left. Don't let them do it." My father stopped reading (I have always thought that this little man who sits on the porch every evening reading the paper is not my father, though I have never dared to tell him). "So you too are carping about the almond tree," he tells me, "Let them chop it down and be done with it." "But I don't want that. I don't want them to chop it down!" I say. "Chop it down, chop it down," he insists. "I don't want to hear one more word." And the bus is really crowded. The heat and the noise are unbearable. A woman carrying a monstrous handbag is incessantly torturing me. I keep watching the exit so she won't be able to get away from me, but I can scarcely see her. I can't even find room for my hands. And to complicate everything, an enormous man is now behind her. What a nerve! If he keeps it up, I'll have to call him to task. But why doesn't she move away? She's being raped in the middle of the bus, and she doesn't even protest. And her home must be at the end of the world. We've already reached the beaches. Here, inside the bus, the heat is intolerable, and that woman keeps harassing me with her handbag and the big man keeps pressing against her, while the council got together at last and one of my aunts said, "We've got to chop it down." And the others, dancing around her, took up the chorus. My mother, unmoved, was smiling from the kitchen. Then suddenly, they all began to shout: "Yes, we've got to chop it down." And I felt the surge of a new hatred. I felt like killing them. And that's why I rushed out to the street. All the streets to the beach look the same, bordered by trees that look alike but seem to be something else, not worth identifying. We walk three more blocks to the seashore. She finally stops by a house identical to all the others. She opens the door and stands there, looking at me. I walk past her with my hands in my pockets, whistling and looking at the tips of my shoes. "Come in," she says, and at that moment I look up; the council is over. One of my aunts goes to the kitchen and brings the ax; the others cheer. And now they all parade into the patio. We begin in the living room rocking chair (there is no time to waste, she says; her family is coming back any minute). She takes my shirt off and leads me to the bedroom. Already in bed, she undresses eagerly and then strips off my trousers and my underwear. The cortege parades across the patio, military style, toward the tree. One of my aunts wields the ax while the others, holding hands, dance in a circle around the trunk. They are silent. Then my aunt grabs the ax with both hands and starts to swing it. With utmost care she first slides her hands over my body, then her lips, and then her teeth; but it's pointless. The first blow of the ax thunders, shattering the afternoon. Birds take flight or seek refuge in the upper branches. My mother wipes the perspiration off her brow, snatches the ax away from my aunt, and, in a rage, begins to strike. The tree is shaken up. My aunts, still whirling around the trunk, now squeal in triumph and jump about, while tearing off the lower branches. Mother swings again; panting, she raises her hands to her hair; in defeat, she sits on the side of the bed and feels her face with her hands. I see her naked and for a moment I have the urge to talk to her. But I don't know what to say. Immediately I stand up, get dressed, and at the doorway I await the brutal comment, the insulting words I deserve. But she says nothing. And that is the worst. I rush out, cross the identical streets, and on Fifth Avenue, I take the first bus. Perhaps I can still come to the rescue. I run into the house, cross the hallway, and bolt out to the patio. There she is, swaying in the late-afternoon breeze. I come up and stare at the trunk in ecstasy. "For today you are safe," I say. And I lie on the ground, on my back. The noise from the birds is quieting down. "I wish there were something I could do. I wish there were something I could do," I repeat. But she says nothing. Her enormous silhouette is projected against the twilight. Then she gives me a few moist leaves that fall on my face, slide through my hands, and end up being caught between my legs. "I wish there were something I could do," I say. And she keeps covering me with her leaves. And this is how we spend the night.

1967

Something Is Happening
on the Top Floor

A bird is singing, perched on
the high electric wires.
If I could, I would also sing,
until my voice gave out.

NOW THE MAN LOOKED down on the street, which appeared to be trapped in a thick network of wires of all sorts. And he started thinking. On the top floor, no city blare reached him to interrupt his thoughts. There were voices rising from the street, and the drone of motors, unintelligible conversations, vituperations, shrieks, music that was not music but clatter adding to the total disharmony, fragmented echoes of marches and demonstrations, gibberish, and whistles. . . . But all that cacophony gradually faded as it passed the lower floors, so that on the top terrace, where he was, only the reverberations from a truly extraordinary noise could reach him, which never happened. . . . A bird was singing, perched on the telegraph or telephone wires or electrical cables. The bird seemed to be glued to the wires, and the man stuck out his tongue and made a threatening gesture, but the bird did not leave and kept on singing. "It doesn't matter; it will be dark soon, and you'll have to go away," the man said aloud. The bird raised the pitch of its singsong, and the man then had to make a great effort to put his thoughts in order within the set time. But the afternoon, *except for that stupid bird,* was a good one for reflection. Standing next to the void, the man felt his ideas come and go; sometimes they stayed for a while playing in front of him, and he saw them coming at him like tiny sunbursts. Once again, it was time to start the story.

A chorus of fixed ideas surrounded the man and left him naked. One of them, very wrinkled and heavyset, jumped at his head from the roof of the building, and the man shrank, turning into a boy. Looking down, he saw himself in the street, running, hawking newspapers from his battered bicycle, and trying to escape from his mother, who was chasing after him with a long mop. He laughed uncontrollably and dreamed he was falling. . . . Up high, ideas would appear and disappear, changing their garb and instruments, sobbing or letting out strange bursts of laughter, dragging themselves on the floor or soaring up in the sky, singing or playing trumpets, shaking their buttocks or making undefinable gestures. It all resulted in a struggle among unusual furies which, in their wild commotion, kept falling into the street and, though invisible, crowding the sidewalks. . . . It was noon, and his mother was sitting on the couch, in the middle of the living room. "Your father is dead," she said when the boy came in. "Your father died," she said. The boy walked to the washstand to wash his hands, but there was no water; the bowl was empty. He stood on tiptoe to see if there were any drops left at the bot-

tom, and the bowl went crashing to the floor, its enamel crack-
ing and chipping off. "Whose father?" the boy asked. The
mother walked over to him and hit him on the head with the
bowl, chipping it even more. It looked totally ruined. So much
so that its screams were heard as the chips were flying away.
"You broke the bowl," said the mother. "You broke it. . . ."
It was that particular time of day when it's neither day nor
night, the time when things change shape, growing bigger or
smaller; the time when all the shadows lying at the bottom of
things, which had been in hiding during the day, can now
escape and stretch until they touch each other and form one
single shadow. From his lookout the man could see the sun
gasping as it sank into the sea in a cloud of vapor. Below, the
boy managed to get across the street without being run over by
the heavy traffic. He slid between two tractor-trailers, caused
several cars to collide, and knocked down an old man, who,
upon reaching the corner, dropped dead in a rage; but the boy
was not hurt. . . . He got home, ran to the bathroom, and to his
horror verified that he was turning into a monster: he was
growing a lot of hair in some unimaginable places. With arms
raised, he walked to the mirror, then ran to the sewing
machine, picked up the scissors, and did away even with his
eyebrows and eyelashes. More at peace, he got out into the
patio. But it was the same the next day, and though he couldn't
tell anybody, he felt an enormous urge to start screaming. . . .
The screams, which never left his throat, reached up to the
man who was struggling with his thoughts on the top floor,
since they were extraordinary sounds. The man, outraged,
threw a cluster of thoughts into the void, and the boy was
transformed. That's how he flashed back to the distressing
period of his adolescence when, without even a dime to go to

the movies, he was smoking in secret and masturbating while looking at a girl with a shaved head. "You have to work," said the mother. "With the English that you know, you could find a job." "Young man," his ad read, "fluent in English, seeks position. . . ." The man above had started pacing. He was walking fast from one corner of the terrace to the other, occasionally leaning over the railing. The city lights were beginning to appear. . . . The following day he received a response from a distillery that made cheap rum—firewater, or *aguardiente,* as people call it. And on his way there, even though he kept telling himself, *Damn it, you are not really going to do that to me and start sweating now,* by the time he arrived, his hands were already dripping wet. He walked between the columns of bottles that obstructed his path, leaving little puddles behind him. But the job did not work out. Yes, it was true he was fluent in English, but that was not the issue. His knowledge of the language was fine, but just broken English would have been enough; what's more, it was not useful to know it too well, and especially not with a Shakespearean accent. Of what use was that Elizabethan thespian diction coming from the throat of a youth whose job was ("no matter how") to persuade tourists from cruise ships to go with him to the firewater distillery, and, once there, to get them drunk? "That's what your job is. To convince them, lure them, drag them here so that they drink our rum. It pays twenty pesos a month. . . ." The terrace clouded over for a moment with hundreds of ideas of all sizes, their membranous wings grazing the man, lifting and shaking him, raising him up to the ceiling and dropping him again to the floor. The man finally got hold of himself and continued walking. Breathing heavily, he cleared the way with his hands and lit a cigarette. . . . The first day he managed to drag along an American tourist, an old teetotaler who thought the boy was taking him to a museum; the next day he carted away two young men who didn't drink but were eager to get to a brothel; on the third day he took with him two very leggy, lanky women who did get drunk, didn't pay, and wanted to have sex with him. On the fourth day he was fired, though he got paid for his three days of work. "He's no good for this kind of work," he heard people say while he hid behind the rows of bottles. "The boy has no drive. . . . We need someone lively who can bring people here, no matter how, and doesn't shy away from anything." *And doesn't shy away from anything. And doesn't shy away.* . . . Now it all became a dizzying return to the same point where his storytelling had started, or rather, to the point where he would end it. . . . He saw himself going in and coming out of one restaurant after another, one drugstore after another, one cafeteria after another. In short, a whole parade of useless and implacable jobs that would only atrophy the beautiful images of the future that he had envisioned for himself in times past. During the whole review of his life, the most peaceful moment was that of the death of his mother. As soon as he found out, he went out into the patio (the place where he used to let off steam when something important happened). "She died," he said. "She is dead," he said. He went back inside and saw her face, so serene: a look that he never had been able to see at all while she was alive. He carried the coffin himself, and paid for the funeral. All his aunts gathered around her tomb, all in black. The scene made him think of vultures devouring a rotten carcass. "Come here, kid," the vultures said, in tears. And he ran away, in between the crosses, and disappeared into the last bustle of the day. Something was telling him that he had been saved. Someone inside him was shouting at him that he had been liberated, that he would no longer need to become an obscure man who bites his lip, and who often gets phone calls saying that everything is fine. And he ran into the crowd. And he wanted to start screaming, "Mother died at last." And he did. And he felt as if an enormous carapace that had been crushing him since the moment of his birth had been lifted. . . . He got married, changed jobs, had children, left the country. He kept on moving from one place to another, trying to escape relentless hunger, and eliminating the possibility of any relief, of any chance of doing a genuine act. Always tied to the damned routine that ruled his time, but waiting. . . . And old age was creeping up even into the most minute corners of his body. The press was reporting exciting stories about the latest events in his country. A revolution, what could that be . . . ? So he returned with all his relatives. Up there, the battle against those membranous beings was coming to an end; the majority of them had fled; others had accepted defeat and were vanishing in the air. Only the very largest ones remained, unforgiving, their beaks threatening. Sounds of children yelling were coming from the living room, and of the mother closing the door to the hallway. "They are back," said the man. And with a gesture, he made all the vermin disappear. But the most powerful ones quickly climbed up the walls, up the drainpipes, and quite intent on staying, they positioned themselves between the man and the door. The clamor of children's voices was no longer audible. Now only the woman was speaking, but he didn't hear her either. "I am sure," he said. "I am fine," he said. "I am at peace." And he shooed away the ideas that, adopting mosquito shapes, were buzzing around his ears and biting him on the neck. With great effort, he delved into the retelling of the present days. He had been able to review all of his life in the grip of those vermin, and now he found himself at peace, with the triumph (was that the word?) that alleviates the horrors of getting old. Again he could hear the children's yells. *I am doing fine. Here is home, my home, and behind the door are my wife and kids. I have a decent pension. Here is home.* And his hands caressed the walls, as if the house were a domestic animal. . . . The voice of the woman could be heard, calling him. "I'm coming," he said, "I'm coming, I'm coming." And he groped in the dark trying to find the door. "This is peace: a home, a pension, and the kind of weather that always remains the same. Always remains the same," he repeated as if trying to accelerate his steps by means of words. "And the kind of weather that always remains the same," he said once more, and stopped. Then he leaned over the railing again. Way down there, beyond the jungle of cables, the rush-hour lights were swarming. . . . There were voices that the man did not hear. Moving like a performer, he passed his feet over the railing and, once on the other side, he held on to it with only one hand. Then he let himself go, without haste, like someone sliding in from the edge of a swimming pool. "Aren't you going to come in?" his wife asked from the dining room as she came out on the terrace. "Oh," the woman said, raising one hand, not to any part of her face but to her neck. Like that she went into the dining room, and in a reassuring manner, began to serve dinner. . . . The man, bursting through wires, flagpoles, and neon signs, was coming down with an impish smile. Shattering the last lightbulbs, he fell headfirst on a car top, and bounced three times. . . . The boy, standing on the sidewalk, saw him hit the ground and smash into pieces. Then he took his battered bicycle, and continued hawking his newspapers, but with a little more verve. He was glad to have watched that spectacle, which he had seen only in an occasional movie when he had money (rarely) for the ticket.

The bird, frightened by the thud, flew away, circling the deep red sky that was already fading slowly into the horizon. The bird finally landed, perching on the telephone wires of a neighborhood street. Its song was heard for a while in the dark of night.

La Habana, 1963

The Parade Ends

To Lázaro Gómez Carriles, witness

NOW SHE'S ESCAPING ME. Again I'm going to lose her in this sea of legs so close together that they seem to blend into a jumble of clothes and compressed bodies, all these bare feet sinking into pools of urine and mud, into mounds of excrement. I'm looking for her; I keep looking for her as if she were (as in fact she is) my sole salvation. But again she is escaping me, the bitch. There she surely goes, miraculously clearing her path, slithering away between the soiled shoes, between bodies so tightly packed they cannot collapse even if they faint, amid the tears and urine, liberating herself from me as she slips away and, at the same time, by who knows what sort of unique intuition, managing to elude being fatally trampled. My life depends on you, my life depends on you, I tell her, slithering along just like her. And I go after her, sinking into the shit and the mud. I continue to pursue her, laboriously but mechanically pushing away bellies, buttocks, feet, arms, thighs; a whole mass of stinking flesh and bones, a whole mélange of screaming, shifting bulges wanting like me to move about, to turn around, to go somewhere else, and causing only greater compression or balancing on the other foot while stretching and convulsing but unable to break through, to take a step, to run, to truly get moving, or accomplish some dis-placement, some advance; all of us, like prey, caught in the same spiderweb that yields on one side, pulls back on the other, and lifts here, without ever permitting a breakthrough anywhere. So people retreat, advance, move backward, for-ward, between knee-bumping, kicking and being kicked, now raising arms, heads, noses high toward the sky in order to breathe, to see something other than the fusion of their own stinking bodies. But I proceed, I have not yet lost sight of her, and I continue pushing away bodies, dragging myself, being hit and cursed, but not giving up, still going after her. On this (on her) I'm betting my life. Life above all, life in spite of it all, life under any conditions, deprived of everything, deprived of you (and in spite of you), in the loud noise now rising between the cries and the singing, because they sing and sing again, the national anthem, no less. Life now, while I go after you, step-ping through the excrement to the tune (or the screaming) of the anthem, their refuge and justification, instant solution, support; and as for the other things (what other things?), we shall see. Now I care only about that lizard, so crafty and cov-ered with excrement, that damned lizard, again scurrying away from me among the thousands and thousands of feet also mired in shit. *Life* ... He had reached again, like so many years ago, that extreme situation in which life is not even a useless and humiliating repetition, but is rather the ceaseless remembering of a repetition that in the beginning was nothing but a repetition; he had reached that place, that ultimate situation, that extreme point at which the fact of being alive stops being a matter to consider, and becomes instead something one cannot even be really sure is true. Standing there, or actually bent over, since his loft did not allow him to stand up straight, he was just staring, in that old room of a hotel that had seen much better days and was now inhabited by people like him, or even worse—screaming creatures with no other concept or principle or dream besides being able, regardless of means or of cost to anyone, to survive, that is, not to end up starving to death. From his motionless position, he was not looking at the past or the future, since both were not merely gloomy, but absurd; he was really looking at the makeshift steps to the "upper floor," that is, to the loft where he could not even walk scrunched up but had to move on all fours so as not to slam his head into the ceiling. There he was, between the front wall by the hallway and the other wall by the sidewall of another building. Now he moved a bit, and his eyes met unexpectedly with his own image reflected in the mirror bolted to the door (kept provisionally closed) that faced the hallway. He was not the same person anymore; he was this other one now. He no longer ran through the savanna or the grasslands. He ran sometimes now, but through the hysterical mob, trying to climb on a crammed bus or to get a number in the line to buy bread or to buy yogurt. So, with effort, he drew back from his image—the present one—to move two body-lengths to reach the other end of his den, his kingdom, and sit on his makeshift seat, also put together in a combination of misery and necessity. It was like a

stool covered by a parody of a cushion. Then, before he could
think about a solution, before he could even think of how to
think of a solution, there was loud noise: the violent scraping
of a kitchen pot, a child's shriek or howl (to give it some name),
the blare of voices from a television at full volume and several
radios, from someone also pounding on the elevator door,
and from a man endlessly yelling out, at the top of his lungs,
at someone who evidently was not in or was deaf, didn't want
to respond or had died; that is, at neighbors, at his fellow
human beings, which made him forget whatever had crossed
his mind like a brief gust of wind, or that he had tried to
conceptualize—what was it, what was it. And as he listened to
the incessant pandemonium, a tremendous calm invaded him,
a pervasive feeling of impotence and resignation that sub-
merged him in a kind of stupor, or inertia, well known to him
for many years. It was an overwhelming sensation of abandon-
ment, of mortal dejection (or consolation), that made him feel
beyond all resistance, all capability and vitality (a quiescence, a
weariness), a certainty of real and irrevocable death. Yes, all of
that was true, except for a saving grace: he had a friend. And
therefore he could still breathe. Not with ease but with a lot
of difficulty, by lifting his head, his nose; by opening his
mouth toward the sky, by raising his arms, too, and separating
himself, for only in this way could he take in a bit of the
entirely contaminated, foul air, and go on, that is, dive back
into the cacophony and the sweaty bodies, and again drag himself through the slippery, heavily trodden muck, pushing away
legs, bundles, feet, trying to get to wherever his friend was,
because he was certain that he was there, of course, in that
mob, somewhere within that mob, as a part of that mob; that
was why he pushed, lifted his head, inhaled, scrutinized the

crowd, and continued pushing bodies and bundles away, without saying "excuse me" (who would apologize in this situation?), and he went on, at times calling out to him, trying to make himself heard over the ruling pandemonium. And the worst of it was that to continue was becoming more difficult by the minute. More people came, they kept coming, more and more people were jumping over the fence to get in. The gate had been closed already, but they were getting in at all costs, kicking and hitting. What a scandal, what an uproar. Through the dust and the shootings they kept coming, climbing up and vaulting the fence: old people, fat women, children and youths, mostly youths, all trying to reach the wire fence, while the rows of soldiers were becoming denser. More policemen, militiamen, people in uniform or in civilian disguise, were coming to stop the others—the crowds outside—from getting close to the fence. It was no longer a police cordon, but a triple cordon of fully armed officers. Now there was machine-gun clatter, and shouts of "Bastard, stop right there!" accompanied by the commotion and howls of those who, right there, in front of everybody, were being gunned down before climbing the fence, before touching it, before even getting close to it. Immediately, many men (soldiers in and out of uniform) hurriedly exited their Alfa Romeos, dragged the dead into their cars, and sped down Fifth Avenue. Now it was not only dangerous for the agitated masses outside who wanted to break the cordon (rather, cordons) and get in by any possible means, but for those inside, also being gunned down. Someone, one of the top dogs, a *pincho,* a *mayimbe,* abruptly stopped his car close to the fence and, enraged beyond control, started firing. Screaming in horror, the masses retreated, although they actually couldn't, squeezing even more tightly against one another, and hiding their heads; they folded back as if trying to recoil into themselves. Anyone who was felled by a bullet, or who had simply slipped, could never stand up again, but would instead have as a last vision the thousands upon thousands of feet crossing overhead again and again, in circular stampede. "The national anthem, the national anthem," somebody shouted. And suddenly, out of the immense mass of people under siege, came a strong, unanimous voice, a loud chant, impudent, out of tune, one of a kind, projected beyond the fence and into the night. *This is absurd, absurd,* he told himself, but for a moment he interrupted his search, he stopped; *absurd, absurd,* he repeated, that anthem again, *absurd, absurd,* but he was crying. . . . Horrendous, it was horrendous, because everything was horrendous, frightening, now, again, and forever and ever; but worse, much worse now, because he couldn't afford the luxury, as before, of wasting time, his own time. His body bent within the narrow, low-ceilinged cubicle, he reviewed and reviewed once again the time he had lived, the time he had wasted, and he stopped there, as always, on the essential, makeshift steps, under the ceiling, also essential and makeshift, before the essential and makeshift table (a vat cover on top of a barrel); makeshift, makeshift, makeshift, everything was makeshift, improvised; and besides, he himself, and everybody else, had to be always improvising and accepting. Listening to improvised and incessant speeches; living in an improvised misery, where even the terror he suffered today would be replaced provisionally tomorrow by a new one, renovated, reinforced, augmented just like that, unexpectedly. Suffering from improvised laws that suddenly fostered crime instead of decreasing it; suffering improvised angry attacks against him, naturally, and against those who lived like him, at the margin, in a cloud, in another world, that is, in a room like this, ten by twelve, makeshift, on a makeshift loft, alone . . . To go out, to go down the stairs littered with garbage (the elevator was never working) and get to the street, what for? To go out was to prove once more that there was no way out. To go out meant to learn again that there was no place to go. To go out was to run the risk of being asked for his ID, for information, and, in spite of his always carrying all of the regime's calamities—ID, syndicate ID, working ID, Obligatory Military Service ID, Committee for the Defense of the Revolution ID—in spite of his being, in fact, like a meek and noble beast, with all the cattle markings that his owner had firebranded on him, to go out meant the risk of failing to look good enough in the eyes of any policeman, who could designate him (just by moral impression) as *an individual of doubtful character, suspicious, not solid-looking, untrustworthy,* which was enough to land him in jail, as had already happened on several occasions. And he knew what that meant. On the other hand, what kind of scene would he find outside but the anatomy of his own sadness, the overwhelming spectacle of a city that was crumbling, of taciturn figures, either evasive or aggressive, all of them starved and desperate as well as harassed? Figures, in addition, already alien to any form of dialogue, any intimacy, any possibility of communication, and simply ready, out of vital necessity, to grab other people's wallets, wristwatches, even eyeglasses from their owners' faces, if they had been imprudent enough to go out with them on, and then to start running, without a word, into the dilapidated surroundings. Besides, it was not completely true—and this was his triumph, his anchor to salvation, his consolation—that he felt, or was, totally alone. . . . And with this consolation, this joy, he remained where he was: one foot on the makeshift steps, face blurred in the ramshackle mirror, head bent so as not to hit the low ceiling of his loft—serene, still, and waiting, because he was sure that his friend would arrive any minute now, as he did every morning. Yes, that was the way it would be; his friend would come. Finally he stepped into his makeshift room and sat on his makeshift seat. But where was he, where was he headed, where could he have gone; yet you must keep moving, he told himself; you must forge ahead, you must find him somewhere, on the roof, up in a tree; he cannot have vanished, he must be in this tumult, within this immense crowd that is growing bigger and becoming more hysterical. Now the people have captured someone, and they are throwing him up in the air and catching him so as to keep bouncing him back up; it's a policeman who had infiltrated their ranks, they say, someone who was trying to lower the Peruvian flag from its pole. And now hundreds of desperate people's arms, thousands of closed fists, are going after him, hurtling him back and forth. Let's lynch him, Execute him, Off with his head, people are shouting, while the man disappears and reappears, to be swallowed again by the sea of desperate people, until he is hurled outside the fence. There the shooting continues, at the trees, in the air, at the cars which from a considerable distance and at great speed are trying to break through the barriers and get closer. I go where the furor is most intense, I look around, and push my way through, I keep searching every anguished face, among those who have fainted, whether from the beatings or because of lack of food, among those who are asleep on their feet. . . . But nothing, nothing, I don't see you, though I know, I know very well, that you're somewhere around here, probably pretty close and also searching for me. We are here, we are both here, though we have not been able to find each other yet, with the threats and the shootings, with the awful smells becoming more intolerable all the time, and with the riots, the beatings, the fights, the conflicts that hunger and desperation, and this melding together, are causing; but at least we're able to scream, now, right now, to scream, to scream. . . . To leave, to get out, that was the question. Before, the concern had been to join the rebels, to seek liberation, to revolt, to go into hiding, to find emancipation and independence. But now, none of that was possible, not because it had been achieved or was no longer necessary, but because now it was not advisable to express any of those ideas out loud, or even in a whisper, and so both of us keep talking while we walk in fear along the Malecón, now practically deserted though it's not yet ten o'clock. The problem is not to say "We must leave." I know that as well as you do, his friend said. The problem, the question, is how to get out. Yes, we agreed, how to get out. Maybe in one, or two, truck inner tubes, you say, with a canvas cover and a pair of oars. And then set out into the open sea. There's no other way out. That's true, that's true, I said, there is no other possible solution. I can get the inner tubes, you say, and the canvas. You have to keep them in your room. My family must not know anything. But that is not the hard part, you said. It's the other stuff. The surveillance. You know there is surveillance everywhere, and one cannot even get near a beach at night. The biggest problem is precisely how to get to the shore with two inner tubes and food and a few water bottles. Yes, I was saying. That's right. First we have to inspect the place, study it, that is, go there without carrying anything, and see which is the best spot. I heard that maybe in Pinar del Río, you were saying. At least the currents are stronger there, they can pull us out, take us far. Some ship will pick us up. They have to; once we're out at sea, someone will detect our presence and pick us up. But listen, I say, maybe we'll get picked up by a Russian ship, or Chinese, or Cuban, and we'll be brought back, except not here, to the Malecón or to the street, but to jail. . . . It's five years now for what they call "illegal exit," you say. And where is the legal exit? I asked. Would it be possible, perhaps, that if we wanted to leave, we could do it normally, as people do anywhere in the world, or almost anywhere? Of course not, you said. But they, they are the ones who make the laws here, and the ones who put us in jail. That's true, I said. Not only is there the problem of getting out to sea, but also of getting to the other side of that sea. Have to get there somehow, you say. Without their finding out that we are thinking about leaving. They, they, I was saying. But no matter how much they watch, they cannot keep track of everything; they can't, even if that's all they do with their lives, watch over us, check on us every minute, nonstop. Perhaps you're right, you said. And on the way back (it was better not to talk about this in my room), we finished rounding out our plan, our escape, our possibility, our attempt, but now she has disappeared again, she sneaked out, slipping out from below, through the mud and the excrement. Changing color, she has escaped from me again. In the crowd someone squeals. A woman jumps about hysterically, putting her hands to her thighs. "A bug, a bug," she says, "a bug crept inside." And the woman keeps on jumping. Until she scurries out of her skirt. There she goes, fleeing again, changing color and trying to hide, the bitch, in between the muddy shoes and bare feet, climbing up someone's thigh, jumping onto somebody else's back, now sliding between the sweaty necks pressed to one another, over the tumult that recedes, forming a single mass on the ground. I go over them too, I step on the face of someone (a woman, a child, an old man, I don't know) who doesn't have the energy to protest, and I go on, crouching on all fours now, sometimes raising a noisy chorus of complaints, besides getting kicked, shoved about, but watching her still, following her, keeping her in sight, now much closer. . . . But they, it was true, they did control everything, watch everything, listen to everything. They had thought of everything. That's why they came very early. I went down in a hurry from the loft, thinking it was you. It was them. In one moment it all happened, it continues happening, it feels as if it had already happened. I had thought about it (expected it) so many times, imagined so often how it would happen, that now, when they come in and say, "Don't move, you're under arrest," and begin their search, I don't really know if everything is happening this instant, if it already happened, or if it keeps always happening. Since the space is so small, they don't need much time for their search. Two of them up in the loft turn everything upside down; one of them stays below, guarding me; the others look under the cushions, in the double ceiling, in the improvised closet. And there they are, of course, the inner tubes and canvas, and something that I didn't even know you had been able to get (which is now the most damaging): a compass. The search is quick and thorough, all done in front of me, but as if I didn't exist. Papers, letters, books, the inner tubes, the canvas, and, of course, the compass, which I didn't even know you had put in the closet; every object at this point becomes evidence, motive, probable cause, degree of guilt. A photo and a foreign pullover become for them convincing proofs, "instruments" of the same crime. They finally order me to take off my shoes in order to inspect the soles of my feet, then ask me to get fully dressed again. "Let's go," one of them tells me, putting his hand on my neck. We leave that way. The hallway is now totally empty, though I know that behind their doors, kept ajar, my neighbors are all there, fearful, watching. A woman who lost an eye when someone threw a stone at her, a man whose arm had been blown away by a bullet, another whose legs are swollen, almost bursting, a woman who presses against her belly and shouts that she doesn't want to have her baby, because when she does, they'll force her out of here; someone who is groping blindly because he lost his contact lenses. "Quiet, quiet, let's see if we can listen to the Voice of America." There are shouts, and more shouts demanding silence, but nobody shuts up; everybody has something to say, something to discuss, some solution, some complaint, some urgent business. "Let the ambassador speak, let the ambassador speak." But nobody listens. They all want to be heard. "We're going to starve to death, going to starve to death. Those bastards want to starve us." There are shouts, and more shouts, and I'm also shouting: I'm calling out to you, pushing away people who are constantly getting angrier, hitting anyone in my way, proceeding through the excrement, the urine, the mangled bodies and the noise (the shooting outside, the shooting again), still looking for you. . . . At night—is it night already? Who can tell whether it is night or day now . . . ? Night, night, it's night. Now it's always night. In the middle of this medieval tunnel and with an enormous lightbulb that is never turned off over one's head, of course it must always be night. Everybody brought down to the same uniform, the same shaved head, the same shout at roll call three times every day. Every day? Or every night? If I could at least get closer to the triple-barred window, I could find out what it really is now, night or day; but in order to get there one must belong to the "ruling class," be one of the "bullies." Little by little, time passes, we pass, I pass. It's not that I'm getting used to it, or adjusting to it, or resigning myself. I'm just still surviving. Fortunately, on your last visit you were able to bring me some books. Light, we have plenty of that here. Silence, silence, that is really something I can hardly remember. But the problem, you tell me, is being able to endure, to survive, to wait. I was lucky they didn't catch me in your room. At least I can bring you a few things. Here is some roasted cornmeal, crackers, sugar, and more books. Time passes, time passes, you say. Time, I say, does it pass? . . . It passes when you know that outside there are streets and trees, people dressed in different colors, and the sea. Visiting time is over. We say good-bye. Going back in, that is the worst moment, when (duly escorted in the all-blue line, heads shaved) we enter the tunnel, the long, narrow, stone vault leading us back to that circular cavern, which incessantly exudes bedbugs, mildew, urine, and the particular steamy smell of excrement accumulating, overflowing; and to that din, that constant shouting of the prisoners, those beatings on the bunks and against the walls, to that powerlessness, that caged violence that somehow has to come out, manifest itself, burst. If only, I think while taking cover behind the last bunk, if only they would kill each other in silence. But this din, this deafening and monotonous exploding, this cackle, this jargon, in which, like it or not, one has to participate, participate or die. Oh, if there were anyone who had a bit of interest in my soul, if anyone would like to have it forever, in exchange I would . . . But it's totally impossible to keep on thinking, with all this commotion, this dissonance, now rising and expanding its offensive. . . . As if struck by a unique plague, the trees have unexpectedly dropped all their leaves; one by one they have been yanked off and swallowed at lightning speed. Now, with their nails, with pieces of wire, with the heels of their shoes, everybody starts to rip the bark off the tree trunks; the roots, the grass, also disappear. "He who hides a piece of bread is playing with his life," I hear someone warn. That is why I'm following you; that's why, and for much more than that. You are my goal, my salvation, my reprieve, my motivation, my love, my big, my only and true love forever. And now once again you are provoking an uproar when you slither inside the pants leg of someone who was sleeping standing up, supported by the crowd. "An ass-fucking lizard," somebody shouts, since in spite of, or because of, everything, people are still holding on to some of their sense of humor. "No, it's a pansy," pipes in someone else. "I drove her away when she was getting to my fly." "It might be a macho," a woman says, "because it got underneath my skirt." "Let's catch her; hey, it's fresh meat." And upon hearing that battle cry, they all jump on you. I, howling out, cross over their heads. I won't allow it, I won't allow it, I won't allow the others to be the ones who get you, even if they kill me (I already see their faces eyeing me furiously, hungry, delirious, crazed); I keep pushing, making my way, coming to get you. "The food, the food." The alarm sounds. Shrieks. Now, forgetting about you, we all try to reach the fence, where they say the guards are beginning to leave small cardboard boxes with food rations. The crowd is growing increasingly unruly, despite some people's efforts to keep order. We know the delivery will be of only eight hundred rations, for more than ten thousand people gathered here now. There are beatings and rioting again, a lot of shouting. For the first time they have saved me, they have saved us, you and me; and so now, more urgently and with free rein, I am coming after you. I arrive. Finally I arrive again at the place I hate so much and nevertheless missed: my makeshift den. Everything seems resplendent. The dilapidated, peeling walls now seem to glisten; the sidewall of the next building looks like solid marble. I touch the improvised seats, the improvised stairs; the few crude furnishings around me all seem new, and I look at them and feel them, I would say, with something akin to love. Five years in that cavern, you remind me. Of course everything must seem wonderful to you. And you also recount all you had to suffer: investigations, persecution, and all the rest, but now we must forget it all and go on, you say. Now we must be under heavier surveillance. That's why, you say, it's best to forget about escape for a while. To pretend you have adapted, and not to tell anyone what you think. When you have to let off steam, talk only to me. Not a word to the others. All this happened to us for not being cautious enough. Yes, I say, though I had never spoken to anyone about the matter. But they are very shrewd, you say, more than you think. They might not have been able to develop the shoe industry or the food production or transportation, but when it comes to persecution, they are masters. Don't you forget it. . . . I'm not forgetting it, I'm not, how can I ever forget it . . . ? They are outside, some in uniform, others as civilians, all of them well armed, beating, abusing, murdering those hidden in trees, in the sewers, in the empty houses, those who are trying to get closer, to get in with us. And now the guards over there are putting the boxes with food (a hard-boiled egg, a bit of rice) at their feet, on the outside of the fence. They feel gratified seeing us inside. When one of us sticks out an arm to grab a box, the guard lifts his foot and steps on the hand, or quickly lands a spry kick in the chest. When somebody screams, the guards' laughter just gets louder, much louder than the screams. If they are more sadistic, or refined, they wait until one of us reaches a box and is trying to take it inside, to beat him until they break his arm. And their laughter is heard again. But you are not among those who, after being shoved and kicked, reach the fence, nor among those now withdrawing their stomped, empty hands. Perhaps you're up there, on the roof of that building, or inside, with the ambassador himself, taking care of those who are very ill, or the women who just had babies, or the elderly. Yes, surely I should have gone there first, because, that's it, you are with the sick, or undoubtedly sick yourself, seriously sick, and that's why I have not been able to find you. Otherwise you would have located me before I could find you. Going back, going back, to recede, to go back between shoves and kicks, and to return, to enter that building by whatever means, going back, going back. . . . I had arrived. Finally I had personally reached that point in which life not only makes no sense at all, but in which it's no longer a question whether it ever did. My tone may sound grandiloquent in the middle of this dilapidated room, but that doesn't make this fact less tragic. And I go on, because one cannot afford even to feel sad. Even sadness itself gets canceled out by the uproar, and by the constant invasion of cockroaches, by the sirens of the patrol cars, by the cries of, What shall I eat today? What shall I eat tomorrow? Yes, even sadness needs its space. At least a bit of quiet, a place where we can keep it, exhibit it, show it around. In hell one cannot feel sad. One simply lives (dies) day by day, I say, I said. And you answered: Write, write about it all, begin writing right now what you are suffering, and you will feel better.

Actually, for quite a while I had been thinking about doing that, but what for? For you, for you yourself, for both of us, you say. And you're right. In a thorough, delirious, and angry manner, I am incessantly letting out all my horror, my fury, my resentment, my hatred, my failure, our failure, our helplessness, all the humiliation, the mockery, the swindles, and lastly, simply all the beatings and kickings, the endless persecution. All, all of it. All that terror goes onto the paper, the blank page, which, once filled, is carefully hidden in the double ceiling of the loft, or inside dictionaries, or behind a cabinet: it is my revenge, my revenge. My triumph. *Jail to bite, jail to shipwreck and never be able to resurface; jail to give all up once and for all, forgetting, not even imagining, that the sea ever existed, and, much less, the possibility of crossing it. . . .* My triumph, my triumph, my revenge. Walking along streets that collapse into sewers that have burst and crumbled; going past buildings to be avoided because they might fall on you; past grim faces that summarily judge you and sentence you; past closed shops, closed movie houses, closed parks, closed cafeterias, some displaying signs, excuses, now covered with dust: CLOSED FOR RENOVATION, CLOSED FOR REPAIRS. What type of repairs? When will such renovation, such repairs, be completed? When, at least, will they start? Closed, closed, closed. Everything closed . . . I arrive, open the countless padlocks and run up the makeshift stairs. There she is, waiting for me. I find her, remove her canvas cover, and stare at her dusty and cold features. I wipe some dust away and caress her again. With my own hands I clean her back, her base, her sides. Desperately happy to be with her, I sit down, run my fingers over her keyboard, and, suddenly, it all starts up. With the tat-tat, tat-tat-tat, the music begins, haltingly, then faster, now at full tilt.

Walls, cathedrals, trees and streets, beaches and faces, jail cells, tiny cells, huge cells; bare feet, pine stands, starry nights, clouds; a hundred, a thousand, a million parrots, low stools, a creeping vine; it all comes back, it all returns, they all attend. The walls recede, the roof vanishes, and quite naturally you float, float, uprooted, dragged off, uplifted; you are carried in arms, transported, immortalized, saved by that subtle, constant cadence, by that music, by that endless tat-tat-tat-tat-tat. . . . My revenge, my revenge. My triumph . . . Bodies armor-clad in excrement, children sinking in it, hands that search, stirring the shit. Hands and more hands, round, slender, flat, bony, palms up, palms down, joined, apart, making fists, closing; scratching hair, testicles, arms, backs; hands clapping, raising, dragging, hanging down in exhaustion; black, yellow, purple, white, translucent after days and days without food; inflamed, bruised, mutilated by beatings from trying to secure a ration box outside the fence where police cars, now with loudspeakers and on constant patrol, blare their thunder endlessly. "Anyone who wants to ask for the protection of the Cuban authorities can do so and return home." And day and night, day and night, the shootings, the thirst, the threats, the hunger, the beatings. And now, unexpectedly, a rain shower is coming down in torrents, dissolving the cloud of dust, blurring the images of trees, cars, tents and military units, soldiers at their posts hiding behind parapets, all on the alert, all surrounding us. . . . A typical spring shower, sudden, torrential. Some people inside try to cover themselves with their hands; others, lowering their heads, seem to crouch as if they wanted to shrink, retract within themselves. For many who are asleep, the rain keeps running down their faces, their foreheads, their closed eyes, without waking them. Some who try to bend down, to seek protection under the others, cause an avalanche of protests, rebukes, and an occasional random kick. I take advantage of the confusion, the moment of calm that the unexpected shower has provoked in the stunned crowd, to make my way, scrutinizing the wet faces, the constricted and soaked bodies that occasionally suffer tremors and pulsations, and I continue, I continue inspecting them, watching them and trying to decipher their dripping faces, in my search for you. I know that here, not far from me, a step away perhaps, is where you are, where you must be. "They want to defeat us through starvation, sickness, terror. This shower is surely their doing, one of their tricks," a woman declares, crazed under the deluge, while she makes crosses and strange signals in the air. . . . And I return, energized, my arguments replenished, my horror. I run up the sordid steps, open the countless padlocks. Fueled up, I climb to the improvised loft. My treasure, my treasure, I'm looking for my treasure, which I am going to expand right now; my vengeance, my triumph, which has been growing and it's no longer just a page, or ten, or even a hundred, but hundreds. Hundreds of pages robbed from sleep and rest, from horror and fear; wrested honestly from the asphyxiating heat, the clamor of the street, of the neighbors; won through a battle against mosquitoes, against perspiration, against the steamy, foul smells coming from upstairs, downstairs, everywhere. Thousands of pages won over the squeals of sinister children who seem to tacitly agree to interrupt in concert with their devilish brawls the moment I sit in front of my keyboard. Pages and more pages conquered out of punches, kicking, beating my head in fury against the wall, out of enraged blows in the struggle against television sets, record players, transistor radios, noisy motors, shouts, jumping about, and pots being scraped, unexpected visitors, unavoidable bodies and figures, incessant blackouts . . . Blows, blows, in the dark, fast, fast, faster and faster, blows, blows, before they come back, fast, fast, more blows: triumphal, victorious in the darkness . . . And again the uproar: beams, searchlights, flares now seem to burst everywhere, illuminating Fifth Avenue and the whole zone as if it were midday. Someone, a taxi driver with a Chevy, has managed to break the barriers, the cordons of guards, and has crashed at incredible speed into the ambassador's own car, which was parked at the entrance. The wounded man finally gets out of his demolished vehicle and begins to drag himself slowly toward the fence, where we watch him pulling at the grass to propel himself. Then the official government cars come forward and direct their headlights at him, while soldiers carrying flashlights surround him, joined by guards, other soldiers, judo experts, policemen from the three cordons around the embassy. They circle him but allow him to continue dragging himself. The driver is very close to the fence now, where everybody, myself included, keeps looking at him. Finally, when his hands are touching the wire fence, the circle of light closes up on him, the men advancing slowly, their guns aimed at him. Two of them bend down to lift him, gripping his belt and shirt, and carry him away. He looks at us and we see him opening and closing his mouth but saying nothing; nothing is heard, though all around, at this moment, there is total silence. . . . Nothing, nothing, there is nothing, not a page or fragment, nor even the latest, the unfinished one, left in the typewriter. I empty the drawers, turn over the mattress, the clothes in the closet, the improvised seats, I pull out the false ceiling, the covering on the improvised stairs; in consternation I examine and shake all the books. Nothing. From all the hundreds of scribbled pages, there is not a trace, not even a vestige of how they disappeared. . . . They, they, of course they did it, you tell me, while I, accepting my defeat, stop turning things over. No doubt they did it, you go on. Then they'll come back and arrest me, I say. Maybe so, maybe not, you tell me, just as worried as I am, though trying to pretend, trying without arguments to encourage me, to console me. Maybe they will not come, you say. Everything was in perfect order, nothing was disturbed. How on earth were they able to get in? Don't be naive, What is it that they can't do? They are the masters of the whole country, of all of us, they know every step you take, what we talk about, and maybe, even what we think. Don't you see? That is why they did it, so that you would know that they know. Don't you realize that what they want is precisely for you to become aware of that? For us to recognize that we are in their power, that there is no escape. That just as they took those papers and no one knew about it, not even you, they can also secretly dispatch you. You could be strangled or hanged somewhere, or you could appear to be a suicide, or to have died of natural causes—thrombosis, heart failure, whatever—and the door and the room, as well as everything else, will remain intact, in perfect order, in its place. And maybe a letter will materialize, composed and signed in your handwriting, as your farewell. . . . He stops talking. For a while both of us remain crouched over the pile of books in disorder. Now he takes a blank sheet of paper at random and brings it to his lips slowly, holding it between his teeth as if it were a blade of grass. Then you tell me, now in a whisper, I don't think they are coming to get you, to get us. This was only a demonstration, a refined showing-off. No more than a proof of their shrewdness, their power, their control . . . And now what are we going to do? I say. Play their game, go lower. Listen to this: play their game or perish. Let's go for a walk, you tell me now, softly. We'll fix all this mess together afterward. And we go out. . . . So at this point he was again where he had been many times before, in the same place, the same extreme, his hand on the makeshift stairs, his eyes contemplating the stark panorama, the four improvised seats, the bolted mirror (at that moment the closest blaring radio became intolerable), but he was still there, at that extreme point, on the edge, in the apparently incessant remembrance of a repetition, cautiously bending down, contemplating the vista that ends abruptly a few steps away: the dilapidated sidewall of the building next door and the old closed-off door leading to the hallway, where now someone, or a group of people, is uselessly calling out at full lung capacity for an elevator that never comes up. They shout and beat the door. What a pounding they are giving the old artifact, the cage, which of course does not respond. Elevator! Elevator! And the beating continues. And again, Elevator! The ruckus continues; it's all noise, but there are no signs of life. . . . So, thinking, commenting in a low voice, protesting, at times with irony but with great caution, they validated their existence only when out of the room, in a deserted spot along the Malecón, on an empty street or in a field, and even so, with both of them watching carefully on all sides. Because the question now, as his friend, his only friend, had told him, was not simply of having to suffer, but of having to praise out loud all the suffering, of having to vociferously support all the horrors, of not writing anything critical or borderline, but finding everything in favor, unconditionally, and leaving the pages carelessly on the improvised table, in a discreet but evident place, in case they came in. And in the afternoons, in a natural, normal voice, not too loud (the enemy is very skilled, very skilled, the other said), which could cause suspicion that they were pretending, the two would comment on the "benefits," the "achievements," the "noble endeavors" of the regime, its endless "progress." They would also read *Granma* aloud. But not so loud, please, or they might think we're poking fun. The opening of the latest Soviet film, *The Great Patriotic War!* (was it this one?), *A True Man!* (or that one?), *Moscow, You Are My Love!* (could that be it?): how marvelous, how many positive elements, a real piece of art . . . But no, not so loud, please, they may suspect, they may realize we're being sarcastic. *We Are the Soviet Men!* Lower, still lower. *They Fought for the Homeland!* . . . Shut up, shut up. *The Ballad of the Russian Soldier!* . . . Sssh. And we applauded. At the block meetings or at the plaza, while we observed how we were being observed with a look of disdain and mistrust or with an ironic, condescending expression on their faces, since they will never be satisfied; not even when, after so much pretending, you may forget your true expression, who you are, your place in the world . . . But at this moment, half-dressed, just a few minutes after getting up, descending the improvised vertical stairs toward the improvised bathroom in that improvised cubicle, bent down between loft and "ground floor," he stopped: suddenly he had the certainty (once more, yes, but always anew) that not only was it impossible for him to get to that box of a bathroom, but he was also unable to take a step through that junk, and moreover, he could not even move his hand from one step to the other (to go down or up his improvised stairs he needed to support himself with his hands). Thus immobilized, he looked not to the past or the future (what was that?), but at the dilapidated boards, at the spots on the wall (was it dampness?), and lastly, unexpectedly but without surprise, at his own image reflected in the mirror. To the tune of that pot again being scraped with a vengeance (coming from upstairs? downstairs? across the hallway?), he was overcome by inertia. And in that din, alienated and helpless, he felt he was finally dissolving, becoming paralyzed, disappearing, no longer pretending defeat in order to gain time, to go on, to be able later to stand on his own, but feeling clearly routed, done for. Right then—at that precise moment—there was a knock at the door. It was he, his friend, knocking as he always did before entering, though he had, of course, the keys to all the padlocks. After closing the door, he whispered in his ear: Haven't you heard? Heard what? That people are entering the Peruvian Embassy. The guards have been withdrawn since yesterday. They say the place is crammed. I'm going there. Let's go, I told him. No, you said. Wait; you have too much of a record. I'll go first and see how things are. And if it's true the place is not guarded, I'll come for you. Wait for me here. And he left. But he could not just stay there on the improvised stairs. He had something to do: get dressed, and wait. And I waited all through midday and all afternoon. Until dusk. In the hallway people were running, sliding, trying not to make noise, something never attempted before; even the radios had been turned off. I open the door, go down. In the street no one is talking, but everybody seems in communication somehow. I hurry to catch a bus toward the embassy. The bus feels more crowded than ever, something hard to imagine. Nearly all are young people. Several even dare to speak openly of their intent: to get inside the embassy quickly. Before they close it. It will surely be closed any minute now, someone next to me says. The problem is to get there, I say; then we'll see. Yes, to get there, another answers. And to stay, because anyone who leaves will get that on his record, besides getting kicked and arrested. And the passengers keep talking. Now I know why you couldn't come back. I've been stupid. I should have realized it sooner; if you didn't return, it's because it was impossible. And you probably thought that if you didn't come, I was not going to be that dumb and stay in my room. Quickly, the problem now is to get in quickly. To find you, to find you fast before you think of coming for me and get arrested, if you haven't been already. And it is all my fault, what an idiot. Quickly, quickly, for I'm sure now you're waiting for me, that you weren't trying to leave me behind, that you thought that if you couldn't come back, I would, of course, come to see what was going on . . . In packs, amid the stone-throwing, the dust and the bullets, people are getting in, we are getting in. All sorts of people. Some of them I know, some I have seen somewhere, but now we are all greeting each other with euphoria, feeling a sincere and mutual connection never experienced before, as if we were all great old friends. People and more people, from Santo Suárez, from Old Havana, from El Vedado, from all the neighborhoods, people and more people, especially young ones, jumping over the fence, dodging the blows or receiving them, running through the frenzy of bullets and the blare of police cars and loudspeakers; people jumping over in a terrorized parade, kicked and shot at, beaten with rifle butts; bodies collapsing, a woman dragging a young child by the arms, an old man using his cane to make way. A motley crowd, jumping over the gate, over the wire fence, already filling the gardens, the trees, even the roof of the embassy building. This way, in the immense cloud of dust, among hands that push and pull, amid shrieks, threats, explosions, we still manage, now in a single impervious mass, to break through the ever-tightening surveillance, and we jump, get in, and fall in with a crowd that can barely move, here, on the other side of the fence, surrounded by a circle of government cars and patrol cars that keeps growing: Alfa Romeos, Yugos, Volgas. All the elite class, the civilian and military top brass, have come in their brand-new cars to see, to try to contain, to repress, to try by any means possible to put an end to this spectacle. To top it all, they have just blocked with their cars and barriers all streets leading to the embassy, and hundreds and hundreds of soldiers dressed in civilian clothes, as everybody knows, have been deployed throughout the zone to prevent anyone from getting close to us. Now a motorcycle policeman skids violently in front of the army ring surrounding the whole embassy. "Bastards," he shouts at us. Then he draws his gun. All of us here recede as best we can, attempting to get away from the fence. The policeman, gun in hand, reaches the fence, jumps over, and lands among us. Frantically he takes off his uniform, wraps the gun in it, and throws the bundle over the fence, to the other side, where they are. Here, inside, there is applause, shouts of "Viva." The cordon around us triples. It's beginning to get dark. The noise we are making acquires such proportions that even the tumult and the shootings outside briefly stop. "They're going to gun us down, they're going to gun us down," a woman suddenly screams. And the massive crowd, ourselves, again tries to retreat any way it can. The trees disappear, the roof of the building disappears. It's all a swarming anthill, people crawling, climbing, eagerly holding on to one another. Screaming. Some are falling, wounded. Panic is now generalized, because somebody is in fact shooting those inside. But that is not what I'm concerned about. I'm making my way back because I need to find you; I must find you, get to where you are, to wherever you may be. In the middle of this terrorized throng, practically without being able to move, and in the dark of night, I must find you, so that you can see that I also came, that I had the courage to get in, that I did not shrink at the challenge, that they could not completely destroy me—destroy us—and that here I am, here we are, making another attempt again. Both of us. *Alive,* still *alive* . . . That is why I don't mind stepping on this human mound that now seems to be asleep, here at the entrance of the residence. Maybe, surely, you are inside. This is the one section that I haven't yet searched, and you must be here, sick, no doubt. The commission in charge of maintaining order tries to stop me, but I push them aside and go in. There are people lying on the floor, the elderly, women on the verge of giving birth, little babies, the infirm; in short, those that were allowed to be here, under a roof. I go on; I go on looking for you, opening doors to rooms, cubicles, pavilions, or whatever damned names they call this hell. "Boy," a half-naked woman says to me, "get out of here, the ambassador is hopping mad because people ate even his parrot." But I keep searching all the compartments. I push open a door to find two bodies entangled in a strange way. I get close to them; mechanically I separate them and look at their faces, which look back at me in puzzlement. I leave. "It's incredible," an old man tells me, his legs bandaged with assorted rags, "to feel like fucking when we have gone without any food for a whole two weeks." . . . I go out again, crossing this sea of people, people about to collapse or barely holding up, tottering, looking for support from one another, and who, if they finally do collapse, can never reach the ground, because it doesn't exist. Covering the ground is the shit, the urine, the feet, all the feet, sometimes standing on others' feet, and sometimes supporting a person's whole body on only one foot. Thus, in this immense jungle of feet trying to move, I move. I keep after you. You're not going to get away from me. You're not going to get away. Don't think, you bitch, that you're going to escape. Definitely not now. Now that no one is even noticing you—well, they can scarcely look at anything—this time you really won't escape me, and I keep on, I keep on trailing her, as she (the sneak) is running toward the fence, toward the outside. But I continue, day and night, scrutinizing all the faces. You could be one of these. Is that you? Are you one of these? Hunger changes faces. Hunger can alter even our own brother beyond recognition. Perhaps you are also looking for me and don't recognize me. Heaven knows how many times we might have bumped into each other without realizing it. Really, are we still able to recognize each other? Fast, fast, we are getting more disfigured by the minute, and it will be more and more difficult to meet, to discover each other. That is why it's best to shout. Loudly. As loudly as possible. Louder than those damn loudspeakers outside. I'm calling you as loud as I can. But if I shout, how am I going to hear you if you're calling for me? I shout; then I keep silent for a moment, waiting for an answer from you, and then I shout again. Though we might not recognize each other, we'll be able to hear each other's shouts, to hear our names, to hear each other's calls. And finally, we'll meet. . . . So I go on shouting in the tumult, which is again agitated now. "Food, food, they are distributing food," people scream. And again the crowd, with renewed miraculous energy, moves toward the fence. It's the same ritual again, the same beatings. "They are going to bring the fence down," someone screams. If this happens, we won't be in Peruvian territory anymore. But the throng of people cannot be contained. Who can make his way through this crush? But I try, and I also push and advance between punches, slaps, kicks. Pushing away their faces, and bodies that roll over, I continue to the end. Now I am sure I will be able to find you. Yes, you must be there, by the fence; that's what an intelligent person like you would logically do, so you could be the first there to get whatever is distributed, the first there to hear whatever they say, and the first to see danger when it comes, and move back. I should have thought of that. Of course that's where you must be. So, pushing and shoving, kicking, biting, dragging myself through this witches' Sabbath of bodies that are also dragging themselves, I finally get to the wire fence and I hold on to it. Nobody can yank me away, damn it. Nobody is going to pull me out of here, I shout, beginning to observe the faces of all those who are managing to get here. But you are not among those who, like me, are now risking their lives to reach the fence. I look and look again at those desperate faces, but, certainly, none is yours. I see bloody hands that don't want to loosen their grip on the wires, but they are not your hands. Defeated, I stop looking at the fence and instead look through, out where the soldiers are, well fed, bathed, well armed, in uniform or civilian clothes, now getting ready to "serve" our food. And I discover you, finally I discover you. There you are, among them, outside, in uniform and armed. Speaking, making gestures, laughing, and having a conversation with someone who is also young, also armed and in uniform. I stare at you again while they begin, you begin, to distribute the small food boxes. Now they (you) go up to the corners, along the sides of the fence. The gun in one hand, the small box in the other. The distribution begins. The uproar and the blows from those next to me are now much heavier than before. They crush me, they want to crush me, they want to stand on top of me to reach one of those filthy boxes being handed out. Idiot, I call myself, while people kick me, climb over my body, use me as a springboard to get up like on a promontory, and desperately stretch their hands over the fence. Idiot, idiot, I call myself; and while everybody is walking over me, standing on me, jumping on me, I begin to laugh out loud, as if all those feet, all those legs covered with shit and mud were tickling me. . . . "That guy has gone crazy," somebody says. "Leave him alone, he might be dangerous," someone else says. And they move away from me, climb down off my body. Outside, the soldiers, also laughing, are methodically distributing the food boxes all along the fence. They place a box on the ground. They stand next to it and wait until someone reaches out for it, in order to smash that hand with a quick stomp. . . . I could right now stretch out my hand and grab that box. Whether they step on my hand or kick me in the chest, I won't starve anyway. So let no one imagine that I'm going to give them that satisfaction. And don't you start thinking I'm going to please you; don't let them think, don't you for an instant dream, that I'm going to eat that shit, that garbage, that filth. And least of all, that I would allow you to step on my hand in exchange for a hard-boiled egg. That is why, in order not to allow them that pleasure, I will remain here, motionless, triumphant, looking at them (at you) out there, playing games with that filth. So here I am, looking at them and laughing, while arms over my head are trying desperately to reach out. Then I actually see you for the first time. I discover you, also there, outside, trying to evade a shiny boot, running, dragging yourself silently across the asphalt and coming in, what a wild idea, with the throng of people, here with us. Here she goes, there she goes, almost in a daze, almost without the energy to keep trying to escape, but still moving, under the bodies, over the hands and faces barely blinking when she crosses them. She can't keep going. She can't keep going anymore after so many hours of trying to escape from me. And now she's stopping as if stunned, her mouth open, over somebody's back, someone who is lying facedown on the ground. She's desperately trying to jump somewhere. . . . I finally get you, you bitch, because even covered with filth, there is no escape left for you now.

1980

Alipio's Kingdom

TWILIGHT SPREADS its incomparable violet hues while Alipio, standing by the balcony railing, becomes almost indistinguishable from the last autumn leaves on the almond tree.

Alipio is motionless, looking at the sun as it descends at the customary slow pace of one who is going nowhere in particular.

The top branches of the almond tree light up briefly. Suddenly, all is calm.

The sky turns darker.

Alipio, who has been awaiting this for a while, rubs his eyes with his hands as if he were trying to clean an opaque glass with an oiled cloth. Alipio's hands are thin and white, and a bit clumsy. His face glows with the declining rays of light.

Alipio grins; night is close. The moment the last trace of day vanishes, he slowly raises his head to look at the sky.

The first stars have just come out. Venus, Alipio utters with a smile. His teeth are short and square, much like a rabbit's.

Gradually the sky becomes incandescent; in a short time, stars in phosphorescent outbursts suddenly appear. Alpha, Alipio says, and looks toward the west. Omega, he says, and now he tilts his head backward so he can look at the highest point in the sky. Ursa Major, he mutters, lifting his arms shoulder high. He's in ecstasy, motionless for a moment; then he turns slowly toward the north to watch an almost imperceptible constellation. That's the Pleiades, Alipio says. But the sky is already a luminous outburst and he does not know where to direct his gaze. On one side of the horizon the Andromeda constellation beams from afar, and Alipio's eyes are helplessly fixed on it; at the other extreme the dazzling white Castor and Pollux exchange knowing winks like inseparable friends. Almost crowning the sky, big Orion glows like a burning tree and only Sirius, the most brilliant star, can outshine it briefly. Alipio keeps turning his head really fast: that's the Global Accumulation of Omega and Centaurus, he says, raising his hands high up as if he wanted to dig his fingers into the constellation. There, the Southern Cross, and Arcturus, the yellowest and most mysterious nebula. He keeps naming the constellations, one by one, even the most insignificant stars that possibly disappeared billions of years ago. Finally he begins to jump up and down on the balcony as if trying to escape up into the sky, raising his hands, running from one side to the other, squealing with pleasure, laughing out loud. Up above, the stars now shine in their maximum opulence; constellations turn at full speed, die out, surge again, are extinguished forever. New stars come to occupy the few vacant spots; radiant comets cross the heavens swiftly or dissolve into a luminous rain over the ocean. Alipio has stopped dancing. In the midst of the translucent night, his body is now rigid. A small noise comes out of his body. Tonight Alipio seems happier than ever before: it's November, transparent and resonant. November, playing all its fanfares in the darkness; making the farthest comets perceptible, and even some in the process of forming. Alipio has spent the whole day running errands. But at dusk he hurries to his room and locks himself up. He would run no errands now for anybody, no matter how much money he was offered. And he stands, waiting for the night, his figure almost indistinguishable among the last autumn leaves on the almond tree. And at dawn, when the last constellation disappears in the wrenching white luminosity of day, Alipio jumps into bed and sleeps two or three hours. He has done this for years and plans to keep doing it. And in the month of November, when Alipio watches the skies, large tears well from his eyes. He jumps from one end of the balcony to the other, grabs the railing with his white fingers, softly touches the leaves of the almond tree. . . . His dearest friends are the luminous Dragon constellation—all of its seventeen sparkling bodies—and Capella, the Charioteer's she-goat. Alipio has not been able to study (the only field that interested him was Uranography, but then he would have needed to abandon real stars to look at their photographs in books). Alipio has no home other than a balcony where he can see all he wants of the heavens, right before his eyes, and that is enough for him. He feels blissfully happy; he stretches up a bit more, and his lizard neck becomes reddish. Alipio's kingdom is now fully on display. Even visible tonight are the faraway constellation of Hercules and the variable Agol, constantly changing color. Alipio feels a renewed joy that makes his throat quiver, reaches down to his chest, and bursts into countless stirrings in his belly. The gravitation of all these luminous creatures way up in the sky above overwhelms him. Suddenly, still looking up, Alipio becomes transfixed. A brilliant point of light spins around the stars, moves away from the constellations, rolls over the heavenly bodies, and lights up the moon. The great luminary keeps descending. Alipio remains ecstatic. An enormous glow, dizzyingly coming down, stops for a moment as if to gather force or take its bearings, and then advances fast toward the earth. All the constellations have disappeared. The moon shows only an edge that soon dissolves in the light. Only the enormous glow is visible. Alipio lifts his hands over his head, grabs the railing, and jumps. He lands on the pavement and, terrified, starts running. The luminary resembles a gigantic red-hot spider in a boiling rage; the flying sparks kill the night birds and seed the clouds, provoking hail showers and ungodly thunder. It stops again as if looking for direction. Alipio keeps running. The luminary is already getting close. The plumes of the palm trees get scorched. The telephone poles and the television antennas become tall but crumbling towers of ashes. Alipio runs toward the ocean intending to jump into the waves: his hands reach the water. He howls: the water is boiling hot; the fish, leaping uselessly, are falling back into the sea. The light keeps descending toward him. Alipio trembles and yells uncontrollably. He runs from the beach and seeks refuge under a bridge, digging his hands into the ground, trying to disappear. The light continues on its way down and discovers him. In the deserted city, it seems nobody will be there to witness the catastrophe. Alipio's ears perceive a sort of hum, which soon intensifies a thousand times, and then it's like a horrifying scream that is not really a scream because it could not come from any familiar creature. For an instant Alipio looks at the approaching fire: it's like hell itself, an overpowering eagerness whose dimensions he could never have imagined. It's not one star; it's millions of them devouring one another, reducing themselves to minute, self-consuming particles. Alipio, yelling at the top of his voice, runs toward the fields. The luminary keeps after him, while the trees go up in a blaze and vanish. A group of cows retreats in terror to the far hills. Alipio goes after them. The enraged animals repeatedly try to gore him, kick him, run him over. The light keeps descending and the heat becomes unbearable; loud squeals keep coming from the shrubs, which crazily uproot themselves, flying up and bursting over Alipio's head. The birds, as if pulled by invisible strings, bump into the light's edge, turning to ashes. Alipio starts running to the thicket, where the taller bushes are wresting themselves from the earth. He holds on tight to the tottering thicker trunks, which, after some wavering, rise with the wind, turning also into ashes. Alipio throws himself on the now bare ground and tries to grasp the earth. He feels vulnerable, and the great luminary quickly discovers his defenseless condition. The sounds coming out of his throat resemble the heavy grunting of an aroused bull or of some ravenous beast suddenly coming upon a cornucopia of fresh food. Alipio begins to lift himself up from the ground. He floats about. The tumultuous luminary seems to reach its crest. Alipio passes out. . . . The first splendors of dawn settle upon the trees. The top leaves of the almond tree shine like polished metal. Little by little Alipio begins to stir, moving not yet consciously. He opens his eyes. He finds himself in the middle of the field, lying in a viscous puddle that bathes his arms, his legs, and has splattered up to his eyes. He tries to sit up. A strange pain runs all through his body. He looks around and notices the sticky goo surrounding him. He wets his fingers in the thick substance and brings them to his nose. Immediately, shaking his hands, he stands up and starts walking. It's semen, he mutters. Angry and saddened, he keeps walking through the bare fields, leaving a wet trail behind.

Twilight spreads its intolerable violet hues while Alipio, standing by the balcony railing, becomes almost indistinguishable from the last autumn leaves on the almond tree. He has been motionless for a while, looking without seeing the people going to and fro on the sidewalk. Precisely at the moment the sun disappears, Alipio, with a quick jump, goes into his room and lies down, covering himself up completely. It's seven o'clock and Alipio, wide-eyed, stares at the ceiling. It's eight, and Alipio, who is perspiring profusely, still has not decided whether to open the window. It's nine, and Alipio thinks it must be almost dawn. It's midnight. The sky is bright with all its characteristic standards. The stars of the first magnitude speed by like the sails of a gigantic windmill. Ursa Major moves in the northern sky and touches David's chariot; the Centaur's tail joins the Southern Cross; the shy Pleiades, all tremulous, advances toward Hercules. At that moment, Capella enters in conjunction with the Charioteer, and the Seven Sisters twinkle next to Orion, which is expanding. Stars in the zodiacal constellations invade the sky and fuse with the cluster of the Pleiades. The variable stars, insignificant comets, and gleams from galaxies that no longer exist dazzle the earth. The sweet constellation of the Unicorn appears for a moment, its white stars barely discernible in the distance. Castor and Pollux, the inseparable ones, are very close. Alpha approaches Canis Minor. Andromeda's great nebula shines bright, transparent and resonant on this beautiful November evening. Alipio's tears surge warmly, run along the sides of his nose, wetting his pillow.

Billions of solitary suns rush about the boundless heavens.

1968

Halley's Comet

For Miguel Ordoqui

> You can never tell
> what will become of you.
> FEDERICO GARCÍA LORCA
> *The House of Bernarda Alba*

VERY LATE ONE NIGHT in the summer of 1891 (that's
right, 1891), when Pepe El Romano runs away with Adela's
virginity, though leaving her behind, everything seems to have
come to a most tragic end for Bernarda Alba's five daughters:
Adela, Pepe's lover, hangs from a noose fastened to the ceiling
of her maiden room; Angustias keeps intact her forty years of
chastity; and the rest of the sisters, Magdalena, Amelia, and
Martirio, are also condemned to spinsterhood or the convent.

But things did not really turn out that way. And if García
Lorca left their story unfinished and unclear, we forgive
him. Being wilder than his own characters—and with good
reason—he followed Pepe El Romano, "that giant, or centaur
perhaps, who huffs like a lion." A few weeks later, though (but

that is another story), poor Federico perished at the hands of that splendid trickster, who, after swindling him out of everything he had and, alas, without even satisfying him first (cruelest of men), slit his throat.

And it happened that while Bernarda Alba was making the arrangements for her daughter's funeral with implacable austerity, the other four sisters, aided by their maid, La Poncia, took Adela down, and by their slapping, shouting, and recriminations brought her back to life or simply out of her fainting spell.

Bernarda Alba's voice was already demanding that the five women open the door when together they decided that a life on the run was a thousand times preferable to living under the fearsome old woman's iron hand. With La Poncia's help, the five sisters jumped out the window and over the garden wall and the corral fence, and when they were already out in the open (and, it must be said, under a splendidly Lorcan moon), the feeling of freedom they enjoyed for the first time made their reciprocal resentments momentarily vanish. The five sisters embraced one another, crying joyously, and swore they were going to leave not only their home and the town but Andalusia and all of Spain as well. After a short stretch La Poncia caught up with them. In spite of her anger, and with a joy that had less to do with the sisters' happiness than with Bernarda Alba's fall from power, she handed them all the house jewels, her own savings, and even the dowry reserved for Angustias's marriage. They pleaded with her to accompany them. She insisted, however, that her place was not on the other side of the ocean but next to the room of Bernarda Alba, whose raging screams "would lull her better"—those were her words—"than the very sound of the ocean."

And they left.

While Federico was expiring, unsatisfied, they were crossing infinite fields of sunflowers, sometimes singing the verses of the dying poet. They left Córdoba and Seville, went through the Sierra Morena, and as soon as they reached Cádiz, bought tickets to Havana, where they arrived a month later, still euphoric and feeling rejuvenated.

They rented a house on Obispo Street near the ocean and, overconfident perhaps, expected future lovers to appear. But with the exception of Adela, the sisters seemed to have no luck with men. Angustias stayed day and night on display behind the wrought-iron window without any success. Magdalena, lanky and thirtyish, would take walks around El Prado Boulevard, but she managed only to have a Dragon Corps lieutenant trample her with his horse and then insult her for obstructing traffic. Amelia, with her stooping back, was only an object of derision and of an occasional stone hurled at her by some young black hoodlum from the Manglar district. Even worse, several youths from the Spanish Volunteer Corp, accusing her of witchcraft and of having offended the king's soldiers, attempted one evening to throw her into the moat at La Fuerza Castle. And Martirio, maybe in hopes that some of Adela's charms would rub off on her, followed her sister's every move, and Adela's belly grew and grew, just like the number of her lovers.

Even though her sisters knew about Adela's very successful amorous adventures in Havana, and resented them, scandal and public condemnation did not erupt until the baby was born. Twenty-five redoubtable men (including six blacks, one Chinese, and four mulattoes) claimed paternity, arguing that the baby boy must have been born premature. The four sisters, who saw Pepe El Romano's image clearly in the face of the newborn, could not bear Adela's disgrace—or rather, Adela's triumph. They declared her wicked and abandoned her. At the same time, they deemed such a dissolute mother unworthy to raise a child and took the baby away from her, though not until they had had him christened José de Alba in the cathedral. Adela wept deeply, but there were twenty-five beaux to console her.

Angustias, Magdalena, Amelia, and Martirio wanted to move to some remote town near the sea. After many inquiries, they finally chose Cárdenas.

This town (now called a city) was minuscule, provincial, and totally boring: very different from old Obispo Street, which had always been full of singing vendors, carriages, smells, women, horses, and men. All of this had made them despair and had forced them to go out often wearing their best clothes, their finest jewelry, and the best cologne. But in Cárdenas nothing of the sort was ever needed. One could not even hear the women talking in the neighborhood, and as for the men, they were always far away, fishing or working the land.

"Being born a woman is the worst curse of all," said Angustias out loud once they were fully installed in their new home.

And right then the four sisters silently promised to renounce every vestige of femininity.

And they succeeded.

Dark curtains covered their windows. They dressed in black and, according to the fashion of their old homeland, covered their heads with gray bonnets that they would not take off even on the hottest days of summer, which in this land seems never-ending. Having abandoned all aspirations for their bodies, they gave in to the stupor of the sweltering heat and to tropical excesses, losing in the process what little was left of their figures. All of them became devoted, with bovine fervor, to raising their nephew.

Naturally, Adela's name was never mentioned in that household, not even by mistake. José (or Pepe, his nickname) was for them, and for all he knew, the nephew they had brought from Spain after the death of his mother in childbirth. The story was no less credible than any other, and because of its pathos, everyone, including the sisters, ended up believing it.

In time they also forgot not only Adela's story—eighteen years had gone by since their arrival on the island—but Adela herself. As for the rest of their former lives, little by little the new calamities they had to face together created new memories for them, or new nightmares: Cuba's War of Independence, which discriminated against them; the big food shortage of 1897; and the birth of the republic, which, instead of marking the end of the hostilities, seemed to bring about incessant rebellions. As if all this weren't enough, some insolent rabble—*human trash,* they called them—had installed themselves everywhere. The sisters got to be known as the "Spanish nuns," and for some reason this *trash* wished they would participate in its noisy and grotesque pandemonium.

So the Alba sisters walled themselves up even more in their chastity, as well as in their approaching old age, devoting their lives to the care of their nephew, who had turned into a shy, handsome youth with curly hair (like his father's). He did not leave the house except to sell in the streets the waxed-paper flowers or the knits his aunts had concocted.

Although the four sisters were the object of envy for some,

the irreproachable, monastic life they led earned them a sort of distant admiration all over Cárdenas. The "Spanish nuns" became the most respected women in town, to the point that someone who wished to praise a woman for her morals usually said that she was "almost as chaste as one of the Alba sisters." The parish priest (they always went to church with their nephew) mentioned them as "paragons of Christian perseverance and morality." Their good fame reached its peak when the priest praised them in his Easter Sunday sermon. It is true that Angustias sometimes assisted the old priest and, accompanied by her three sisters, dusted the altar and swept and washed the church floor with such discipline that it seemed the spirit of Bernarda Alba was supervising her. But it must be recognized that they did these chores not out of obligation or hypocrisy, but out of true devotion.

The four sisters interrupted their monotonous lives only for their Sunday outings to the shore. Dressed in black to their ankles, in their best finery, including black parasols, they would visit the rather desolate Cárdenas seashore. There in the sand, between the water and the rock formations, they would stay sometimes for over an hour like strange, gigantic crows mesmerized by the ceaseless churning of the ocean. Before dusk they would start for home, enveloped in the violet light that seems unique to the region. They looked as if they were returning from a fiesta. José would wait for them sitting on the porch with the proceeds from the day's sales, which were more substantial because it was Sunday. As they walked into the house, they would glance with a certain discreet pride at the small plaque that they had placed by their door some years before: VILLA ALBA, FLOWERS AND HANDMADE KNITS.

There was every indication that those women's lives,

increasingly more devout and silent by the day, produced an almost unhealthful piety, so that their every move was dictated by church bells.

It is also essential to take account of their nephew's behavior. Solitary, shy, conservatively attired (that is, asphyxiating in those black suits), he had no social contact with the outside world other than what was strictly necessary for selling the merchandise that provided the family income. He was eighteen years old, and nobody had yet seen him with a girlfriend, or with any friend. He did not seem to need any more love than the distant, maternal love offered by his aunts. And this shared love was also enough to fulfill the lives of the four women. Certainly none of them still thought of—the words are La Poncia's—what it was "to feel a lizard between her breasts." Much less of having once felt—the words are Martirio's—"a sudden sort of blaze inside."

It is true that you can never tell what will become of you, but in Cárdenas everything pointed to a peaceful end for the Alba sisters, or at least one very far removed from exaltation or scandal.

Something quite unexpected and unique would have to happen to extricate those lives from the ecstasy of their own renunciation. That is precisely what happened. An extraordinary event occurred during that spring of 1910. Halley's comet visited the earth.

We are not going to enumerate the hair-raising catastrophes that the press claimed would take place on the planet with the arrival of the comet. It is all well documented in the libraries. Suffice it to say that the most popular writer of the moment (today justly forgotten), Señor García Markos, obviously also considered himself an astronomer and had authored such books as *Astrology for the Ladies* and *What the Señoritas Should Know about the Stars,* not to mention *Love in the Times of the Red Vomit.* He also published a series of articles that within weeks had spread all over the world, and in them he proposed with a fair amount of scientific verbosity that as the comet's tail entered the earth's atmosphere, this would become contaminated (and "rarefied") by a deadly gas that would bring to an end life as we know it because, and we quote, "the combining of atmospheric oxygen with the hydrogen in the comet's tail will inevitably cause immediate asphyxiation." This preposterous bit of information (preposterous now, forty years after its publication) was taken very seriously, perhaps for its being so uniquely dramatic. On the other hand, as a hypothesis it was not easy to disprove: the comet, according to García Markos, was getting closer to the earth each time around. And who was to know? That very year could be the end. This pseudoscientific writer also insisted that the end of the world would bring plagues of centaurs, griffins, igneous fish, outlandish viscous birds, phosphorescent whales, and other "monsters from outer space," which, as a result of the collision, would fall on this planet accompanied by an aerolite shower. And all of that was also taken at face value by most people. Let us remember that those times (like any other) were backward and there was little to distinguish stupidity from innocence, and lack of restraint from imaginativeness.

The Cárdenas parish priest welcomed with fanatic fervor the apocalyptic predictions of Señor García Markos and all his followers. In an inspired and fatalistic sermon, the priest openly foretold the end of the world: a classic finale, just as the Bible had announced, with the earth enveloped in flames. Naturally, this end was being brought about by the continuous chain of excesses and impious acts committed throughout history by the human race, which had made the divine wrath overflow at last. The end was not only imminent but well deserved. This, however, did not prevent many of the citizens of Cárdenas (or surely, of other locations) from devoting themselves to the construction of underground shelters in which to peremptorily seek protection until the ominous comet had moved out of our orbit. But it is also true that some of the people in Cárdenas, instead of taking precautions against the disaster, brought it on themselves in advance by committing suicide. The municipality has preserved desperate letters from mothers who, rather than wait to face the universal conflagration, chose to go ahead of it, together with all their progeny.

The priest, of course, condemned the suicides as well as the construction of shelters to escape the end. Both, he declared in another sermon, were acts of sheer arrogance, pagan and even illegal, since their intention was to elude divine justice.

On their way home from this sermon, Angustias, Martirio, Magdalena, and Amelia met their nephew in the garden, where he had just built a refuge big enough for fifty persons.

"Close that hole right away," said Angustias slowly but implacably.

Over their nephew's protests, the four sisters replaced the soil. When the job was finished, Martirio began to replant all the vegetation that Pepe had pulled out.

"Sister," reproved Magdalena, "don't you understand that all of this is already useless?"

Martirio, who was holding up some young gardenias, began to whimper.

"Let's go inside," commanded Angustias, pushing her sisters. "Come on. Don't you see you're making a scene? What will the neighbors say?"

"And don't you realize that this doesn't matter either, anymore?" answered Martirio, drying her tears.

Angustias seemed to hesitate for a moment but quickly recovered, saying, "Perhaps our last actions will be the ones that will count the most."

And the four sisters went inside.

It was already late afternoon.

The ominous evening of April 11, 1910, was approaching. The encounter between Halley's comet and the earth, and therefore the end of the world, was expected in the early hours, shortly past midnight.

It must be pointed out that, in spite of the priest's fervent and constant sermons, some in Cárdenas still refused to heed him. Even though they were convinced that the end would come that night, those people did not devote themselves to repentance and prayer, but just the opposite. For their last hours on earth, they decided to have a ball. Early that afternoon groups of drunken youths began roaming the streets. Besides causing quite a ruckus, unheard of in that town, they sang bawdy songs and used shameless language. These people were joined by some women who until then had led more or less conventional lives. Sometimes this din even interfered with the litany of prayers headed by Angustias and echoed by her sisters.

In the middle of all the noise they heard a carriage stop in front of the house and, a few seconds later, someone knock at their door.

"Don't open the door!" Angustias shouted, without letting go of her rosary beads.

But the knocking became more insistent, so the four sisters, escorted by José de Alba, decided to go and see.

They opened the door with extreme caution, and there, in front of them, was Adela. She was wearing a magnificent evening gown of green taffeta adorned with red lace; white gloves; a red mantilla over her head; and a splendid pair of suede ankle-length boots. In her hands she carried a beautiful fan of peacock feathers and a sequined purse, both of which she hurled into the corridor so that she could embrace her sisters. But they stepped back in horror. Adela, unflappable, entered the house swaying her hips and gesturing to the coachman to bring down her luggage, a monumental trunk full of excellent wines, Baccarat glasses, a gramophone, and an oil painting that was an oversize portrait of Pepe El Romano.

"It seems that I am the only Christian in this family," she said as she came into the sitting room. "I am not forgetting you at this critical moment. And besides, I have forgiven you."

"But we haven't," Angustias countered.

"Well, my dear, then I don't know what your religion is," retorted Adela, taking off her shoes, "if even at a moment like this you are incapable of forgiving your own sister."

As she glanced at the rosary Angustias still held in her fingers, it seemed to her a strange object, almost a nuisance.

"My dear sisters," said Adela, full of emotion and taking advantage of the confusion her last words had caused, "I have come because this is the last night. Don't you see? The only night left in this world! And just as we escaped together from that other world of ours, which we hated, I would also like for us to abandon this one together. Our lives have been so different here, but never, not even for a day, have I forgotten you!"

If she intended to say more, the fact is, she couldn't. Her head sank into the red tulle tufts of her skirt, and she broke down, sobbing.

Martirio came to her first and, kneeling, embraced her legs. Quickly Amelia and Magdalena joined her, crying as well.

Finally Angustias took her hand and, pointing to José de Alba, spoke to Adela. "Here is your son. You don't have much time to explain to him who you are."

"That will not be necessary," said Adela. "He is already a man and can understand it all."

"A man, already a man," José de Alba gleefully told himself, and could not keep his cheeks from turning red.

"A man," repeated Adela, "and a very handsome one, like his father."

After asking the coachman to take care of the horses, she walked to the large trunk and began to unpack. She placed the glasses and a few bottles of wine on the table, took out the oversize portrait of Pepe El Romano, and, before anyone could raise an objection, hung the splendid canvas (it had been done by Landaluze) on the sitting room wall.

At the sight of his image, the Alba sisters were suddenly transformed.

"Yes," Adela continued, lovingly looking at the portrait and then at her son, "he has his father's good looks, though he's more handsome. And to think that I have come to know you precisely now, just as the world is coming to an end. A corkscrew! I need a corkscrew!"

"What did you say?" Angustias asked, surprised at the sudden shift in Adela's train of thought.

"Yes, dear, a corkscrew. Or are we just going to sit here waiting for the end of the world without even a glass of wine?"

Angustias began to object. But Martirio was already there with the corkscrew.

"Where did you get that?" Magdalena asked in amazement. "We have never used it in this house."

"You haven't used it because you never cook. But how do you think we open a bottle of wine vinegar?"

"My dear sisters! I cannot believe this!" interrupted Adela, filling the glasses with an excellent red wine. "The world is coming to an end and you argue about a corkscrew. Take your glasses of wine and let's go to the garden to watch the comet."

"It won't appear until midnight," said Amelia.

"Obviously you are behind the times," answered Adela. "At midnight is when the world ends, but the comet can be seen after sunset. Haven't you read the newspapers from Havana?"

"We never read that sort of thing," Angustias protested.

"Your loss," said Adela, "and it is too late to remedy that."

With that, she reached for her son, who was watching her enthralled, and led him by the hand into the garden.

It was a splendid evening, an exceptional tropical night, the kind that can be particularly enjoyed in Cuba. A pale luminosity seemed to come from the land and from the sea. Each tree seemed to be contained in its own halo. In that small town still innocent of electricity, the sky was illuminated as if by some rare candlelight. All the constellations, and even the most remote stars, were sending out a signal, a message that was perhaps complex, perhaps simple, but now already impossible to decipher. The May Cross (though it was April) could be clearly seen; the Seven Sisters were unmistakable; and reddish Orion, distant but familiar, was twinkling. A spring moon rose over the ocean, leaving a track of light that dissolved in the waters. Only a body like a celestial serpent interrupted the harmony of the sky. Halley's comet was making its appearance in the peacefully scintillating immensity of the astral canopy. Then, in a clear but remote voice, Adela began to sing:

> *Girls and women in this town,*
> *Don't keep your shutters down.*
> *The reaper of roses is near,*
> *Seeking a bloom for his ear.*

And suddenly, as if a powerful impulse held back for many years had been let loose, her sisters joined in the chorus:

> *The reaper of roses is near,*
> *Seeking a bloom for his ear.*

They kept singing, and Adela, who had had the foresight to bring with her a bottle of wine, refilled their glasses.

> *Girls and women in this town,*
> *Don't keep your shutters down.*
> *Let's get married by the sea,*
> *By the sea, by the sea.*

Once more the glasses were emptied. Then Adela started to speak.

"Yes," she said, pointing toward the comet, "that ball of fire that is crossing the skies, and that in a few hours will annihilate us, is the ball of fire that all of you"—and unsteadily she now pointed to her four sisters—"all of you have between your thighs, and because you did not put it out at the appropriate time, it now flares up, seeking its just revenge." They started to protest, but Adela kept talking and served them more wine. "That ball of fire is like the embers Bernarda Alba would have stuck into Librada's daughter to punish her for having behaved like a woman. Sisters of mine! That ball of fire is you, who did not want to quench the fire of desire, as I did, and now you are going to burn for all eternity. Yes, it is a punishment. Not for what we did, but for what we did not do. And you still have time! You still have time!" Adela stood shouting in the middle of the garden, her voice mingling with the songs that the drunks waiting for the end were singing in the street. "You still have time, not to save your lives, but to gain admission to heaven. And how do you get to heaven?" she asked, already inebriated, standing by the gardenias. "With hate or with love? Through abstinence or through pleasure? With sincerity or with hypocrisy?" She tripped, but José de Alba, who had been transformed into the sheer image of Pepe El Romano, kept her from falling, and she, in gratitude, kissed him on the lips. "Two hours! We have only two hours left!" she shouted, looking at her handsome silver watch, a gift from a Dutch beau. "Let's go inside the house and pass our last minutes in loving communion."

The six figures staggered into the sitting room. The tropical heat made them, with Adela's help, abandon most of their clothes. Bonnets, gloves, overcoats, skirts, even petticoats vanished. Adela herself helped her son part with his bowler hat, his necktie, his shirt. She led him—both of them half-dressed—to Pepe El Romano's portrait and proposed a general toast. They all raised their glasses.

"I don't know what's going to happen here," Angustias said without a hint of protest, leaning on her nephew's arm to steady herself.

"Wait a second," Adela said, and, walking to her trunk, she took the gramophone out and placed it on the center table. The whole house immediately vibrated with the voice of Raquel Meller singing a popular ditty.

It was not necessary to organize couples. Angustias started dancing with Pepe, Magdalena danced with Amelia, and Martirio led Adela, who, getting rid of her blouse, confessed that she had never grown accustomed to the tropical heat.

"I did not snitch on you to Mother because of love for Pepe El Romano," Martirio said, as if someone had asked her. "I did it because of you."

"I suspected that," Adela answered. And the two women embraced.

Because the drunken clamor in the street was now deafening (there was only an hour and three minutes left before the end of the world), they decided to close the windows, draw the curtains, and play the gramophone as loud as possible. As they danced around, someone turned off the lights. And the whole house was illuminated only by the stars, the moon, and Halley's comet.

When Raquel Meller sang *"Fumando espero"* (Smoking While I Wait for You)—and according to their calculations, there were only forty-five minutes until the end of the world—Adela opened the door and signaled the coachman to come in. A handsome freed slave from the Santa María district, he was overjoyed at the invitation. Wasting no time, he happily shed his livery and leather boots.

Before the gramophone needed rewinding again, both José de Alba and the coachman were embracing the five—by now scantily dressed—women one by one. The glasses were filled again, and all of them, practically naked, devoted themselves to making love under the enormous portrait of Pepe El Romano.

"We're not going to wait for the world to end inside these four walls," said Adela. "Let's go out."

The five Alba sisters, without a stitch on, were soon out in the street, accompanied by José, still in his drawers, and the coachman, who had only his spurs on.

As long as the sky keeps turning (and we trust it will never stop), no one will hear the kind of screaming that was heard in the streets of Cárdenas that night. The coachman—cued, it is fair to say, by Adela—possessed the five women one after the other, followed immediately by José de Alba, who made a masterly debut. Finally, many bumpkins (as Angustias called them) joined the cavalcade, repeatedly mounting all the women, who evidently were not ready to stop yet. Only Martirio occasionally took advantage of the confusion to escape from the arms of some ruffian and go for Adela's breasts. A bit later the two sisters (and now there were only fifteen minutes left before the end of the world) went inside the house and came back right away carrying Pepe El Romano's portrait.

"Now we can go on," said Adela, as she placed the painting facing the stars.

There were only five minutes now before Halley's comet reached its central position in the skies.

And so it did. And then it continued on its trajectory. And

it disappeared over the horizon. And the sun rose. And by noon, when the Alba sisters woke up, they were amazed to see themselves, not in hell or in paradise, but in the middle of the main street in Cárdenas, totally in the buff and still embracing several farm laborers, and a coachman, also buck naked. José de Alba, who seemed as youthful as ever despite his many sexual encounters, emerged once more from the sweaty bodies. The only thing that had disappeared in the confusion was the portrait of Pepe El Romano, though nobody had noticed.

"Well, well, so the world didn't end," said Adela, half-asleep. Stretching, she convinced her sisters that the best thing to do was to return home.

The procession back was led by Angustias, whose fifty-eight-year-old bare body was in the sunlight for the first time; next came Magdalena, arm in arm with the coachman; behind them, Amelia, with someone who said that he was an unemployed carpenter; and at the rear of the retinue, the tight trilogy of Martirio, Adela, and José. In this order they walked through their garden, perfumed as usual by the gardenias, and went inside the house.

But before going in, Adela pulled out the plaque by the door that read VILLA ALBA, FLOWERS AND HANDMADE KNITS, and that same afternoon she replaced it with a more colorful, shining one that said HALLEY'S COMET.

Halley's Comet became one of the most famous and prestigious brothels in all Cárdenas, as well as in the whole province. Experts in these matters declare that it could have competed with those in the capital, Havana, and even with those in Barcelona and Paris. For many years it was splendidly serviced by its founders, the Alba sisters, well educated and generous matrons like none you can find at present (1950).

They knew how to blend love and love of money, pleasure and wisdom, tenderness and lust. But here we must fall silent, because as Knights of the Order of the New Galaxy and as astronomers decorated by the Municipality of Jagüey Grande, we are sworn not to disclose any more details about these ladies' lives. We can only bear witness and, with ample experience in such matters, state that none of them died a virgin.

Miami Beach, January 1986

Blacks

BLACKS WERE not black anymore. They were extremely white. Perhaps for the sake of tradition, or due to a resentment more powerful than reason or even than triumph itself, whites, who were totally black and in full power, were still calling blacks blacks and persecuting them into extinction, notwith-standing the fact that blacks were now indisputably white. It happened at the End, after the Fifth Superthermal War ("The Necessary War"), and during the consolidation of the Great-Universal-Liberated-Monolithic Republic, that the per-secution of blacks reached its peak and caused them all to perish. The hunt had been really spectacular. The invisible flamethrowers, the sound waves that cut bodies asunder, the disintegrators that reduced them to minute luminous particles and cast them into the air, the superatomic rats, and, most fiercely, the pack of supersonic hounds we acquired from our enemy, the Seventh Galaxy, under a merciless treaty that almost totally ruined us, helped dispatch the persecuted in record time, far exceeding the expectations of our Ministry of Harassment. During the deceitful dawns (fortunately abolished now), and coming from the indefatigable cauldrons, from the areas of conveniently contaminated air, from the metallic talons of the beasts of prey, from everywhere, we were forced to hear their howls, at last forever silenced. Of course, in those glorious battles there were numerous titans, numerous decorated fighters, and many who perished but were honored as well. The list of unsung heroes—the patriotic soldiers that most of us tend to forget, the illustrious dead, the children imbued with hate and courage—that list is almost as endless as our infinite empire.

Before ending this document, I would like to put on record the following curious fact. It's about the brief life history of a repressor of blacks, of one of our most bloodthirsty enforcers. It has been said that he alone eliminated from this sacred domain the highest percentage of blacks. In spite of the grand truce, without him and the heroic attitude of our soldiers, women, and children, it has been said, such perfect extermination would not have been feasible. And some of those despicable creatures would still be found up to our times, lurking in remote corners and wandering amid the debris.

"Great Superfirst Repressor of the First and Eternal Great Empire!" he shouted under the far-reaching columns of the Superfirst Repressor Palace. "I have exterminated all the blacks!"

Then the Great Sun—our Great Superfirst Repressor—
came out on the Superfirst balcony.

"You are mistaken," said our Superfirst Excelsitude,
raising his excelsiors: "One still remains."

And taking out his permanent disintegrator, he eliminated the repressor.

When he fell, kicking strangely, we could all bear witness
to the color of his skin: it was repulsively white. There was no
doubt: he was black.

I still remember his screaming, and how he met his end.

La Habana, 1973

Traitor

I AM GOING to speak fast, just as it comes. So don't expect much from your little gadget. Don't think you're going to get a lot from what I tell you, and that you are going to patch it up, add this and that, make it into a big opus, or whatever, and become famous on my account. . . . Though I don't know, maybe if I speak just out of my head, it might work out better for you. It might go over better. You could exploit it more. Because you are the devil. But since you're already here, and with all that paraphernalia, I'll talk. A little. Not much. Only to show you that without us you are nothing. The ashtray is over there, on top of the sink, use it if you want. . . . What a show, impeccable shirt and all—is it silk? Can you get silk now?—but you'll have to stand there, or sit on that chair with the ruined cane seat—yes, I know it could be repaired now—and you can start asking me.

And what do you know about him? What does anyone know? Now that Fidel Castro has been ousted, well, overthrown, or he got tired, everybody is talking, everybody can talk. The system has changed again. Oh, now everybody is a hero. Now, everybody was against him. But then, when on every corner, day and night, there was a Block Surveillance Committee always watching every door, every window, every gate, every light, and every one of our moves, and every word, and every silence, and what we heard on the radio, and what we did not, and who were our friends, and who were our enemies, and what kind of sex life we had, and what kind of letters, and diseases, and dreams . . . All of these were also being checked. Ah, I see you don't believe me. I'm an old woman. Think whatever you want to. I am old, and out of my mind. Keep thinking that way. It's better. Now it's possible to think—oh, you don't understand me. Do you not understand that then one could not think? But now you can, right? Yes. And that in itself should make me worry, if there were still something that could make me worry. If you can think out loud, you have nothing left to say. But listen to me: they are still around. They have poisoned everything, and they are still around. And now anything that is done will be because of them, either for them or against them—not now, though—but because of them. . . . I'm sorry. What am I saying? Is it true I can say whatever I please? Is it true? Tell me. At first I couldn't believe it. And I still can't believe it. Times change. I hear talk about freedom again. Screams. That is bad. Shouts of

"Freedom" usually mean just the opposite. I know. I saw. . . .
There must be a reason why you came, looked me up, and
you're here now with your little machine.

It works, doesn't it? Remember that I'm not going to
repeat anything. There will be plenty of people to spin their
tales. Now we'll have the testimonials, of course, everybody
has a story to tell, everybody makes a big fuss, everybody screams, and everybody was—isn't that nice?—against
the tyranny. And I don't doubt it. Oh, but then! Who didn't
have a political badge, awarded, of course, by the regime?
Make sure you find out, didn't your father belong to the militia, didn't he do voluntary work? *Voluntary,* that was the word.
Even I, when Castro was thrown out of power, almost got executed as a *castrista.* How awful! What saved me were the letters I had written to my sister, who was living in exile. What if
I didn't have them anymore? She had to send them back to me
fast, or else I would be dead and gone. And that's why I haven't
dared go out of the house, because some, a lot, of that still
exists. And I don't want to get any closer to it. I . . . so you are
asking me to speak, to contribute, to cooperate—I'm sorry,
that's not the way you say it now—with whatever I know,
because you intend to write a book or something, with one of
the victims. A double victim, you will have to say. Or triple. Or
better, a victimized victim. Or better still, a victim victimized
by the victims. Well, you'll have to fix that. Write whatever
you want. You don't need to give it to me for approval. I don't
want to see anything. I'm taking advantage, however, of this
freedom of "expression" to tell you that you are a vulture.
Turkey vultures, we called them. Have they all been eliminated? No longer needed? What wonderful birds! They used
to feed on carrion, on corpses, and then they soared into

the skies. And what was the reason for their extermination? Didn't they clean up the island under every regime? And how they gorged themselves. . . . Perhaps they got poisoned by eating the bodies of those executed by justice—is that still how you say it?—that is, by you. . . . Listen, will you bring that machine closer to me? Quickly, because I'm in a rush, and I'm old and tired. And to tell you the truth, I've been poisoned too. This machine—is it working?—was very popular, though people usually never knew when it was being used. . . . Today you tell me what you're going to do and why you have come to see me. We talk. And nobody is watching at the corner, right? And nobody will come and search my house after you're gone, right? Anyway, I have nothing else to hide. And is it true I can say whether I'm for something or against it? Right now I can, if I want to, speak against the government, and nothing would happen? Maybe. Is it so, really? Yes, everything is like that now. Right there on the corner, they were selling beer today. There was a lot of noise. Music, they call it. People don't look so scraggly or so angry anymore. There are no more slogans on the trees. People are going out, I see it, and you can get genuinely sad, with your own brand of sadness, I mean. People have food, aspirations, dreams (Do they have dreams?), and they dress in bright colors. But I still don't believe this, as I already told you. I've been poisoned. I have seen . . . but, oh, well, we should go straight to the point, which is what you want. We cannot waste any more time. Now we have to work, right? Before, the main thing was to pretend you were working. Now we have aspirations. . . . It's a simple story. Yes, of course. But anyway, you won't understand these things. Practically nobody can anymore. These things can't be understood unless you have experienced them, like almost everything. . . .

He wrote some books that should be around somewhere. Or maybe not. Maybe they were burned during the early dismantling of the regime. Then, at the very beginning, of course, those things happened. Inherited bad habits. I really know it's been difficult to overcome all these "tendencies"—can you still call them that? All those books, as you know, spoke well of the deposed regime. However, it's all a lie. You had to go to the fields, and he went. Nobody really knew that when he was working like a maniac, he was not doing it out of loyalty to the regime, but out of pure hate. You really had to see the fury with which he broke the lumps of earth, how he sowed the seeds, weeded, dug. Those earned the big bonus points then. Oh, God! There was such hate in him while he was doing everything and contributing to everything. How much he hated the whole thing. . . . They made him—he made himself—"a model youth," "a frontline worker," and they awarded him "the pennant." If an extra shift of guard duty was needed, he would volunteer. If one more hand was needed at the sugarcane harvest, there he went. During his military service, was there anything he could say no to, when everything was official, patriotic, revolutionary, that is, inexcusable? And even out of the service, everything was compulsory. But by then it was worse, because he was not a youth anymore. He was a man, and he had to survive; that is, he needed a room, and also, for instance, a pressure cooker; and, for instance, a pair of pants. Would you believe me if I told you that the authorization for buying a shirt, and being able to pick it up, involved political privilege? I see you don't believe me. So be it. But I hope you always can do that. . . . Since he hated the system so much, he spoke little; and since he didn't speak much, he didn't contradict himself, while others did, and what they said one day, they had to retract or deny the next—a problem of dialectics, people called it. And then, since he didn't contradict himself, he became a well-trusted man, a respected man. He would never interrupt the weekly meetings. You had to see his attitude of approval while in reality he was dreaming of sailing, traveling, or being somewhere else, in "the land of the enemy" (as it was called), from which he would fly back carrying a bomb; and right there at the meeting—just like so many that he, ominously, had attended and applauded—in a plaza full of slaves, he would drop the bomb. . . . And so, for his "exemplary discipline and dutifulness in the Circles of Study" (that was the name given to the compulsory sessions on political indoctrination), he received another diploma. He would be the first one, when the time came, to read from *Granma*—I still remember the name of the official newspaper—not because he was really interested, but because his hatred for that publication was such that in order to get it over with quickly (as you would with anything you abhor), he would read it right away. When he raised his hand to donate this or that—we donated everything in public—how he secretly laughed at himself; how, inwardly, he exploded. . . . He would always do volunteer work for four or five extra hours—and pity thee if you didn't! He did his compulsory guard duty with a rifle on his shoulder, and the building he was protecting had been built by the former regime—he was protecting his own hell. How many times had he thought of blowing his head off while shouting "Down with Castro," or something like that . . . ?

But life is something else. People change. Do you know what fear is? Do you know what hatred is? Do you know what hope is? Do you know what total helplessness is? . . . Take care of yourself, and do not take anything for granted, don't trust anything. Not even now. Even less now. Now that everything seems trustworthy, this is precisely the time to mistrust. Later it will be too late. Then you will have to obey orders. You are young, you don't know anything. But your father, no doubt, was in the militia. Your father, no doubt . . . Don't take part in anything. Leave!—can one leave the country now? It's incredible. To leave . . . "If I could leave," he would tell me, he would whisper in my ear after coming home from one of those everlasting events, after three hours of cheering. "If I could leave, if I could escape by swimming away, since any other way is impossible, or soar above this hell and get away from it all . . ." And I: *Calm down, calm down, you know very well that is impossible; fragments of fingernails is what the fishermen are bringing back. Out there, they have orders to shoot point-blank, even if you surrender. Look at those searchlights. . . .* And he himself at times had to take care of those same searchlights, and clean and shine the guns, that is, to watch over the tools of his own subjugation. And how disciplined he was, how much passion he put into it. You might say he was trying to create a cover-up through his actions, so that they would not reveal his authentic being. And he would come home exhausted, dirty, full of slaps on his back, and badges of honor. "Oh, if I had a bomb," he would then tell me, or rather whisper into my ear, "I would have blown myself up with it all. A bomb so powerful that there would be nothing left. Nothing. Not even me." And I: *Calm down, for goodness' sake, wait, don't say anything else, they can hear you, don't spoil everything with your rage. . . .* Disciplined, polite, hardworking, discreet, unpretentious, normal, easygoing, extremely easygoing, well adapted to the system precisely for being its complete opposite—how could they not make him a member of the Party?

Was there any job he didn't do? And he was fast. What criticism didn't he accept with humility? . . . And that immense hatred inside, that feeling of being humiliated, annihilated, buried, unable to say anything and having to submit in silence. And how silently!, how enthusiastically!, in order not to be even more humiliated, more annihilated, totally wiped out. So that someday, perhaps, he could be himself, take revenge: speak out, take action, live. . . . Ah, how often he wept at night, very quietly in his room, in there, the next one on this side. He wept out of rage and hatred. I shall never be able to recount—it would take more than a lifetime—all the vituperations he used to rattle out against the system. "I can't go on, I can't go on," he would tell me. And it was true. Embracing me, embracing me—remember that I was also young, we were both young, just like you; though I don't know, maybe you're not so young: now everybody is so well fed. . . . Embracing me, he would say: "I can't take it any longer; I can't take it any longer. I'm going to cry out all my hatred. I'm going to cry out the truth," he whispered, choking. And me? What did I do? I used to calm him down. I would tell him: *Are you insane?*— and I would rearrange his badges. *If you do it, they are going to shoot you. Keep on pretending, like everybody else. Pretend even more than the others, make fun of him that way. Calm down, don't talk nonsense.* He never stopped performing his tasks dutifully, only being himself for a while at night, when he came to me to unburden his soul. Never, not even now when there is official approval, and even encouragement, did I ever hear anybody reject the regime so strongly. Since he was in the inner circle, he knew the whole operation, its most minute atrocities. Come morning he would return, enraged but silenced, to his post, to the meeting, to the fields, to the raising of hands to volunteer.

He accumulated a lot of "merits." It was then that the Party "oriented" him—and you don't know what that word meant then—to write a series of biographies of high officials. "Do it," I would say to him, "or you will lose all you have accomplished until now. It would be the end." And so he became famous— they made him famous. He moved away and was assigned a large house. He married the woman they oriented him to. . . . I had a sister in exile. She used to come, though, and visit me. Very cautiously, she would bring his biographies under her arm. And she told me the truth: those people were all monsters. . . . Were they? Or were we? What do you think? Have you found out anything about your father? Have you learned anything else? Why did you choose precisely this tainted character for your job? Who are you? Why are you looking at me that way? Who was your father? Your father . . ." At the first opportunity, I'll leave," he used to tell me. "I know there is strict surveillance, that it's practically impossible to defect, that there are many spies, many criminals on the loose; and that even if I manage to, someone shall murder me in exile. But before that I shall speak out. Before that, I will say what I feel, I will speak the truth. . . ." *Calm down, don't talk,* I would tell him—and we were not that young anymore—*don't do anything crazy.* And he: "Do you think that I can spend my whole life pretending? Don't you realize that going so much against myself I won't be me anymore? Don't you see that I'm already but a shadow, a marionette, an actor who is never off the stage, where he only plays a shady character?" And I: *Wait, wait.* And I, understanding, weeping with him, and harboring as much, or even more, hatred in me—after all, I am, or was, a woman—pretending just like everybody else, conspiring secretly in my thoughts, in my soul, and begging him to wait, to wait. And he managed to wait. Until the moment came.

It happened when the regime was overthrown. He was tried and sentenced as an agent of the Castro dictatorship (all the proofs were against him) and condemned to the maximum punishment, death by shooting. Then, standing in front of the liberating firing squad, he shouted: "Down with Castro! Down with tyranny! Long live Freedom!" Until the full discharge silenced him, he kept on shouting. Shouts that the press and the world defined as "cowardly cynicism." But I— and please write this down, just in case your machine is not working—I can assure you that this was the only authentic thing your father had ever said out loud in his whole life.

Havana, 1974

End of a Story

For Juan Abreu and Carlos Victoria,
triumphant, that is, survivors

THE SOUTHERNMOST POINT IN THE U.S. That's what
the sign says. And how could we say that in Spanish? *El punto
más al sur de los Estados Unidos.* But it's not the same. It's too
long and lacks precision, strength. In Spanish it's not so clear:
there is no word as exact as "southernmost." However, in
English, that "southernmost point" is absolutely clear, with
those †s sticking up at the end: the world ends right here; once
you leave this "point" and go over the horizon, all you'll find is
the Sargasso Sea, the ominous ocean. Those †s are no letters
but crosses, markers—look at the way they stick up—clearly
indicating that behind them lies death, or even worse, hell.
And that's how it truly is. But anyway, we're already here. I
finally managed to get you here. I would much have preferred

that you had come on your own, and had sent your smiling photo by that sign to me, to the other edge of the Sargasso Sea (so everybody over there would have died of envy, or of rage), and that you could have spit, as I'm doing now, on these waters where hell begins. Anyway, I would have liked you to stay here, on this unique key, a hundred and fifty-seven miles from Miami and only ninety miles away from Cuba, right in the middle of the ocean, sharing the same sea breeze, the same ocean hues, almost the same landscape, but none of the horrors. I would have liked to bring you here—but not having to practically drag you here like this—and not precisely so that you would lose yourself in these waters, but so that you would understand how lucky you were to be this far from them. Despite my insistence—or perhaps because of it—you were unwilling to come here. You thought that what attracted me to this place was merely homesickness, the nearness to our island, and the loneliness, the discouragement, the sense of failure. You never understood anything—or maybe, in your own way, you understood too much. Loneliness, homesickness, memories—call it what you will—I feel all of that. It makes me suffer but, at the same time, I get some pleasure from it. Yes, I enjoy it. Above all, what makes me come here is the sensation, the certainty, of experiencing a feeling of triumph. . . . To be able to look southward, to look at that sky, which I hate and love so much, and to throw punches at it; to raise my arms and laugh out loud, while I can almost hear from over there, from the other side of the sea, the anguished, muted cries of all those who would like to be here like me, cursing, shouting, hating, and being really lonely; not like over there, where even being alone is persecuted and is enough to land you in jail for being "antisocial." Here you can lose your way or find it and nobody gives a damn where you're going. And that, for those of us who understand how that other system works, is also a blessing. You thought I wouldn't be able to see the advantages here and make use of them; that I couldn't adapt. Yes, I know what you said. That I wouldn't ever learn a word of English, that I wouldn't write even a single line more, that once here I would have no more themes or plots, that even my most constant demons would be dying out when faced with the unavoidable spectacle of the supermarkets and of 42nd Street, or with the desperate need to find a place for myself in one of those towers around which the world turns, or with the certainty of knowing that there are no more secret files on us, and that we are no longer a cause of concern for the state. I know everyone thought I was finished, done for. And that you yourself had gone along with the system's maneuvers. I'll never forget how you laughed with a tinge of mockery and sad satisfaction every time the phone rang, and how you relished every opportunity to criticize my lack of discipline, my indolence. When I told you that I was settling down, adjusting, or simply surviving, and thus gathering stories, plots, you looked at me with pity in your eyes, sure that I had perished among the new hypocrisies, the inevitable relationships, the perversions of success or the intolerable gush of words, words. . . . But listen to me: it didn't turn out at all like that; look, twenty years of pretending, of forced cowardice and humiliation don't dissolve just like that. . . . I'm not going to forget how critical you were, always observing me, ready for disapproval, surely expecting me to break down and join the anonymous masses going through the noisy, frozen tunnels or the hostile streets, buffeted by the winds of hell. But that didn't happen, you hear? Those twenty years of shrewd hypocrisy, of repressed terror, kept me from going under. That is also why I have dragged you here, to make sure you are clearly defeated and at peace—maybe even happy—and to prove to you, I can't hide my pride, that you are the one who buckled under.

As you can see, this place is pretty much like Cuba, or rather, like some places over there. Beautiful places, no doubt, that I will never visit again. Never! Did you hear me? Not even if, after the regime falls, they beg me to come back to have my profile stamped on a medal or whatever; not even if my presence is crucial for the whole island not to sink; not even if the red carpet is rolled out right from the airplane exit to the execution wall where I am to parade martially on my way to discharge the grace shot in the dictator's head. Never! Did you hear me? Not even if they beg me on their knees. Not even if they crown me with a laurel wreath as they did with La Avellaneda. Or name me beauty queen of the district of Guanabacoa, the one with the most generous overpopulation of ass-fuckers . . . I meant that as a joke. But what I said about not returning, that's dead serious. Are you listening? You're different, though. You don't know how to survive, how to hate, how to forget. That is why when I saw, a long time ago, that there was no cure for your homesickness, I wanted you to come here, to come to this spot. But, as usual, you did not pay any attention to me. If you had, maybe I wouldn't have needed to be the one to bring you here now. You were always stubborn, human, and sentimental. And one has to pay dearly for that. . . . Anyhow, like it or not, you're here now. Can't you see? These streets are meant for people to walk on, and there are sidewalks, passageways, arcades, tall wooden houses with festooned balconies, just like over there. . . . We're not in New York now, where people shove you without looking at you or apologize without touching you; we're not in Miami either, where there are only horrendous speeding cars in asphalt pastures. Here everything is on a human scale. Like in the poem, there are female figures—and male ones too—sitting on the balconies. They are looking at us. People gather on street corners. Can you feel the breeze? It comes from the sea. Can you feel the proximity of the sea? It's our same sea. . . . Young people are walking around in shorts. There is music. You can hear it all over. Here you won't suffocate in the heat or freeze in the cold like up there. We're very close to La Habana. . . . I always asked you to come, I invited you. I told you about the little ocean drive and promenade, and the seawall, not like the one over there, of course, because it's here; and the trees, and fragrant sunsets, and stars in the sky. But I couldn't manage to convince you to come, and worse yet, I couldn't even convince you to spend some time here, so that you could also begin to appreciate the things available for your enjoyment up there. At night, walking along the Hudson, how many times I tried to show you the island of Manhattan as it really is, an immense, electrified medieval castle, an enormous light, well worth exploring. But your soul was somewhere else: over there, in a remote, sunny neighborhood with stone pavements, where people hold conversations balcony to balcony and when you walk around, you understand what people are saying, because they are you. . . . And what could I gain by telling you that I also wanted to be there, to be riding the noisy, crowded bus that's probably crossing the Avenida del Puerto right now, or to be strolling through La Rampa or going into a public urinal when surely the police are about to arrive and ask me for

my ID? But listen to me: I'm never going back, not even if
world survival depends on it. Never! Did you see that guy who
just passed by on a bicycle? He looked at me. Quite intently.
Haven't you noticed it? Here people do look you in the eye. If
they like what they see, naturally. Not like up there, where
looking at someone seems to be a crime. Or like over there,
where it *is* a crime . . . "Anyone who purposely looks at another
individual of the same sex will be condemned to . . ." Hey!
Another guy also looked at me. And now you really can't
argue anymore. Cars stop and honk their horn; suntanned
young men stick their heads out the windows. "Where to?
Where to?" They'll take you wherever you say. The truth is
we're already in the middle of Duval Street, the "hottest"
street, as we used to say over there. . . . That's also why (I won't
deny it) I wanted to bring you here, so you'd see how the young
men still look at me, and not think of your friendship as a gift,
a favor granted that I must try to preserve by all means, so
you could see that I have my admirers here just as I had them
over there. I think I already told you that. But you seemed not
to care about any of this: neither about the possibility of being
betrayed, nor even about the possibility (always more interesting) of an act of betrayal. . . . I kept talking to you, but your
soul, your mind, whatever it is, seemed to be somewhere else.
Your soul, why didn't you leave it over there together with
your ration book, your ID, and the latest issue of *Granma*? Go
for a walk in Times Square, be daring and wander through
Central Park, catch a train and enjoy the real Coney Island. I'll
take you. Better still, I'll give you the money to go. You don't
even need to go with me. But you wouldn't go out, or if you
did, you came back right away. It was too cold or too hot. You
always had an excuse to keep you from seeing what was right

in front of your eyes. To keep on being somewhere else . . . But take a look: see how those people go out in spite of the weather (there's always bad weather here), see how those people brave the storm; a lot of them are also from other places (where they belonged), places they can't go back to, places that maybe don't exist anymore. Listen: homesickness can also be a kind of consolation, a sweet suffering, a way of looking at things, and even of enjoying them. We can only triumph by resisting. Our only revenge is surviving. . . . Get yourself a new pair of jeans, a pullover, some boots and a leather belt; shave your head, wear leather clothes or tinfoil, put a ring on your ear, a groovy ring around your neck, and a spiky bracelet on your wrist. Go out on the street in a Day-Glo loincloth, buy yourself a motorcycle (here's the money), go punk, dye your hair sixteen different colors, and find yourself an American black lover, or try out a woman. Do whatever you want but forget about Spanish and about everything you ever mentioned, listened to, or remember in that language. Forget about me too. And don't ever return.

But in a few days you're already back again. Dressed as I suggested, in boots, jeans, pullover, and leather jacket. You drink a cold soda and listen to the tape recorder that you could never own over there. But you're not dressed that way, you are not drinking the soda that you could never have over there, and you are not listening to that tape recorder because you don't really exist; those around you don't acknowledge your presence, don't identify you or know who you are, or even want to know; you are not part of all this and it makes no difference whether you dress in that getup or in a potato sack. With just a

quick look at your eyes I knew that was how you were thinking. And I couldn't tell you that I too was thinking like that,
that I too was feeling that way. No, not that way, but a lot
worse. At least you had somebody: you had me, trying to console you. But what arguments can one wield to console someone who still lacks an undying hatred? How can one survive
when the place where one suffered the most no longer exists
but it's the only place that keeps one going? Look—I insisted
because, as you know, I'm pigheaded—now for the first time
we're human beings; I mean, we can hate, we can offend
people openly without having to go cut sugarcane for it. . . . But
I think you weren't even listening. Wearing elegant sport
clothes and looking in the mirror, you see only your own eyes.
And your eyes are looking for a street where people walk softly
swaying their hips, and enter a park where there are statues
you recognize and there are figures, voices, and even bushes
that seem to recognize you. You're about to sit down on
a bench, you sniff around a bit and you feel a mysterious
transparency in the air, the fresh sensation of a recent rain-
fall, of foliage and rooftops, freshly washed. Look at the
balconies where clothes have been hung out to dry. The old
colonial buildings seem like brand-new floating sailboats. You
go down. You want to lean over one of those balconies and
look at the people down below, who in turn look up and greet
you; they recognize you. *A city of open balconies where clothes
hang out to dry, a city of sun and sea breeze, with buildings billow-
ing that seem to be sailing.* Yes! Yes! I would interrupt you, a
city of propped-up, dilapidated balconies and a million eyes
watching your every move, a city of cut-down trees, of whole
palm groves sold for export, of water pipes without any water,
of ice-cream parlors without ice cream, of markets with empty

shelves, of closed-down baths, of forbidden beaches, of overflowing sewers, of incessant blackouts, of prisons that prolifer-
ate, of buses that don't run, of laws that make all life a crime, a
city—do you hear me?—of policemen and compulsory slogans. And what is worse, a city suffering all the calamities that
these calamities bring about. But you, you stayed there, floating, trying to go down and lean on that propped-up balcony,
wanting to go down and sit in that park where surely there
will be a police raid tonight. Go south! Go south! I told you
then—I repeated again—sure that in a place that resembled
the old one, you were not going to feel out on a cloud or anything like it. Go south! I say, turning off the lights in the apartment to keep you from continuing to look at yourself in the
mirror; go somewhere else instead. . . . To the southernmost
point in this country, all the way to Key West, where so many
times I've invited you and you refused, just to annoy me!
There you could find places like, or better than, your own:
beaches where the water is so clear you can see through to the
bottom, with houses surrounded by trees and people who do
not seem to be in a rush. I'll pay for your trip, and for your stay.
And you don't have to go with me. But as usual—without saying a word, without accepting the money either—you go out,
we go out into the street. You walk ahead of me, down Eighth
Avenue. You turn on 51st Street. Feeling more and more disso-
ciated, you enter the Broadway maelstrom; birds darken the
violet skies and perch themselves on the roofs of the National
Theater, the Isla de Cuba Hotel and the Inglaterra, the Cam-
poamor Theater, and the Asturian Social Center; they band
together and take shelter in the only ceiba tree in Fraternidad
Park or in the few remaining, and severely trimmed, trees in
Havana's Central Park. The Capitol is all lit up, and so is the

Aldama Palace. Young people stream along the sidewalks past the Payret Theater and between the lion statues on Paseo del Prado toward the Malecón seawall promenade. The beam from the Morro Castle lighthouse shines on the waters of the bay, on the people crossing over toward the docks, on the buildings down Avenida del Puerto, on your own face. The balmy weather at sunset has brought almost everyone out on the street. You see them, you're almost there with them. Invisible above the few trees, you observe them, you listen to them. Disturbing the birds, you're now watching from the towers of La Manzana de Gómez; you move up a little to see the city all lit up. Hovering along the shore, you feel the music coming from transistor radios, you hear the conversations (the whispers) of those who would like to take the leap across the sea, you watch how the young people walk. If they raised a hand, they would almost touch you without seeing you. A ship is coming into port, slowly sounding her horn. You hear the waves crashing against the seawall. You notice the salty smell of the ocean. You contemplate the slow, glimmering waters in the bay. From the Plaza de la Catedral, the crowd of people disappears into the narrow, badly lit streets. You descend, you want to mingle with the crowd. You want to be with them, to be them, to touch that corner, to sit on precisely that bench, to pull off that leaf and smell it. But you're not there; you see, you feel, you listen, but you cannot mingle, participate, go all the way down. Propelling yourself from a lamppost, you want to land and immerse yourself into the life of that stone-paved street. You jump. The cars—particularly the taxis—keep you from moving ahead. You wait with the crowd for the light to change to WALK. You cross 50th Street and you seem to be swallowed by the lights of the Paramount Plaza, of the Circus Cinema, the Circus Theater, and the huge neon fish from Arthur Treacher's; you're already under the gigantic billboard advertising today *Oh Calcutta!* in Arabic and in Spanish. You walk with the crowd either crammed or scattered around, and voices hawking hot dogs, instant photos for a dollar, roses that "glow" thanks to a battery concealed on the stem, sweatshirts with heavy logos, reflecting sunglasses, fake jewelry, shish kebabs, frozen food, plastic frogs that croak and stick their tongue out at you. Now the caravan of taxis has turned all Broadway into a dizzying yellow river. Burger King, Chock full o'Nuts, Popeye's Fried Chicken, Castro Convertibles, Howard Johnson's, Mellon Liquors, you keep walking. A man dressed as a cowboy behind a makeshift table shuffles some cards deftly, inviting people to play; an Indian woman, in full Hindu dress, is selling aphrodisiac scents and incense, spreading flares and smoke to prove the good quality of her products; a magician, wearing a top hat and surrounded by a big crowd, tries to introduce an egg into a bottle; another magician, in close competition, promises to hypnotize a rabbit, which he displays to his audience. *Girls! Girls! Girls!* a mulatto in tight short pants shouts by a lighted doorway, while a cheerful, aging drag queen proclaims from a high perch her mastery in the art of palm reading. A flamboyant blonde in a bikini tries to take you by the arm, whispering something in English into your ear. In the midst of the crowd, a door guard with two loudspeakers announces that the next performance of *E.T.* will be starting at nine forty-five, and a black man, dressed all in black, with a high, black collar and a Bible in his hand, shouts his gospel, while a mixed chorus, led by Friedrich Dürrenmatt himself, chants "Take Me and Lead Me by the Hand." Someone hawks half-price tickets for the Broadway show

Evita. Another woman, severely dressed in a long skirt and long sleeves, offers you a little book with *21 Amazing Predictions.* Erotically charged young men of various skin colors, wearing spandex pants and patting their promising sex organ, dart by roller-skating in the opposite direction we're headed. A bunch of multicolored balloons goes up from the center of the crowd and vanishes into the night, while a band of musicians, brightly attired and carrying marimbas only, breaks into a glorious polyphonic concert. Someone dressed as a wasp comes up to you and hands you a piece of paper that will allow you to eat two hamburgers for the price of one. *Free love! Free love!* recites a uniformed man in a loud, monotone voice, distributing cards to passersby. The sidewalk is suddenly populated with purple umbrellas that a tiny woman is selling for only a dollar, while predicting an imminent storm. A blind man with his dog jingles some coins at the bottom of a jar. A Greek is selling china dolls with one tear on their cheeks. TONIGHT FESTA ITALIANA, the big-screen neon sign announces now from the tower at One Times Square. Opposite Bond's and Disc-O-Mat, you cross the street and look at the shop windows, full of all kinds of merchandise, from a dwarf orange tree to inflatable dildos, from an Afghan comforter to a Peruvian llama. *Yerba!* someone tells you in blatant Spanglish. They all parade by in front of you, openly offering their merchandise or freely expressing their wants and wishes. On O'Reilly Street, on Obrapía, all along Teniente Rey, Muralla, or Empedrado Street, on all the streets leading to the sea, there are people out for a stroll, in search of some cool sea breeze after another monotonous, asphyxiating day full of unavoidable responsibilities and insignificant, unfinished endeavors, small pleasures (a cold soda, a pair of well-fitting shoes, a fresh tube of toothpaste) that they couldn't satisfy, or big dreams (a trip abroad, a large home) too dangerous even to suggest. And there they go, seeking at least the open skies on the horizon; ill-fed, wrapped in look-alike, shabby clothes, and wondering *Will there be a long waiting line at the soft-ice-cream parlor?* or *Will the Pío-Pío chicken place be open today?* Faces that could be your own face, whispered complaints, curses never expressed in words; all signs and gestures that you understand so well because they are also your own. A loneliness, a misery, a futility, a humiliation and resentment, all of which you also feel. A great many calamities that, if shared, would make you feel less alone. From the arcades of the Palacio del Segundo Cabo you attempt again to submerge yourself in the crowd, but you don't reach the street. You look at them. You share their misfortune, but you can't be there also to share their company. The siren of an ambulance dashing by on 42nd Street paralyzes all the Broadway traffic. Unperturbed, you cross Times Square slowly in the sea of cars; behind you, I almost catch up with you. The Avenue of the Americas, 5th Avenue toward the Village, you keep going through the multitude, a sullen look on your face, an expression of dejection, helplessness, isolation. But listen, I feel like tapping on your shoulder to ask you, What other city, besides New York, could tolerate us? Or what other city could we tolerate? . . . The main public library, the ostentatious shop windows of Lord and Taylor's, we keep walking. On 34th Street you stop at the Empire State Building. Notice how perfect my English pronunciation is! Did you hear me? Up to now, all the words I have been saying in English were pronounced beautifully, do you hear me? I don't want you to start making fun of my accent or put on that other expression, that condescending, weary look that you sometimes show me. Of course you don't make any faces now; maybe nothing interests you anymore, not even making fun of me, not even telling me, as usual, that I'm wrong. Anyway, I wanted to bring you here before we say good-bye. I wanted to come with you on this trip. I want you to get to know the whole town, I want you to see I was right, that there is still a place where one can breathe freely, where people look at us with desire, or at least with curiosity. Don't you see? There's even a Sloppy Joe's, just as good—what am I saying? This one is much better than the one in Havana. All the famous artists have been here. Day and night there is music and you can enjoy the musicians (if for nothing else, for having a good look at them). Here, Hemingway didn't have to worry about old age. There are lots of young men, all of them in beachwear, barefoot and shirtless, suntanned, and showing or suggesting that what they know is their greatest treasure (and they're so right). No wonder Tennessee Williams set up his winter barracks here; he'll certainly find no lack of soldiers. Did you see the stained-glass windows in that house? "Old Havana" style, they call it. And that gallery with the wooden swings? Chez Emilio is the name of the place. At least there's something Latin. Look! There is a San Carlos Hotel, just like the one we have on Zulueta Street. Here at the aquarium, we're only steps away from the docks and the harbor. There is a Malecón here too, not so long and not so high, but with the same sea breeze, well, more or less. . . . Oh, yeah, I know it's not the same, but everything here is on a smaller scale and rather flat, and those wooden houses with their balconies look like dovecotes, or dollhouses, and these streets are not like the ones over there, and this crappy harbor can't compare with ours. You don't have to remind me, you don't have to start your litany again. I know these beaches are no good and that the air is hotter, that there is no Malecón or anything like it, and that even this Sloppy Joe's is much smaller than the one over there. But look, look and listen to me, pay attention to what I'm saying: that one no longer exists, and this one is here, with music and drinks and young men in spandex. Why do you have to look at people that way, as if they were to blame for something? Try to fit in with them, to talk like them and move like them. Try to forget and be them, and if you can't, listen, enjoy your solitude, because homesickness can also be a kind of consolation, a sweet suffering, a way of looking at things, and even of enjoying them. But I knew there was no use repeating the same old song, that you wouldn't listen to me, and besides, I wasn't even sure about all my babbling. That's why I decided to follow you in silence through the long lobby of the Empire State Building. We took the elevator, and still in silence, we went up to the top floor. On the other hand, at that point you hadn't the slightest need for conversation: a group of Japanese (or were they Chinese?) going up with us were talking so loud you wouldn't have been able to hear me. We reached the observation deck. The crowd scattered to the four corners. I had never gone up the Empire State Building at night. The view is really breathtaking: rivers of light flowing all the way out into space. And look up: you can even see the stars. Did I say "almost touch them"? It doesn't matter, you wouldn't have heard anything I said, even if you were by my side as you are now. Anyway, you leaned out over the railing into the void, looking at the sparkling city. I don't know how long you stood there. Maybe hours. The elevator was coming up empty and going down full of (apparently) happy Japanese (or were they Koreans?). Someone near me was speaking in French. I felt the childish

pride of being able to understand his inane words. From
behind the glass of the upper lookout, a beautiful blond boy
was watching me. To my surprise, he made an ample, charm-
ingly obscene gesture. Yes, he did (don't think it was merely
vanity—or senility—on my part); though later, I don't know
why, he stuck his tongue out at me. I didn't pay much attention. The temperature had suddenly gone down and the wind
had become almost unbearable. By now we were alone in the
tower and what I wanted most was for us to go down and have
something to eat. I called you. In response, you signaled me to
join you by the railing. I don't remember your saying anything.
Did you? You simply called me with urgency, as if to see something extraordinary and therefore fleeting. I leaned over. I
saw the Hudson River widening, extending out of sight. The
Hudson, I said, how huge! What an idiot! you said, and kept
staring: the blue ocean was breaking against the Malecón. In
spite of the height, you felt the crashing of the waves and
the incomparable freshness of the sea breeze. The waves were
breaking against the cliffs of the old Spanish fortress, El
Morro, refreshing the Avenida del Puerto and the narrow
streets of Old Havana. All along the lighted seawall, people
are walking, or have stopped to sit for a while. Fishermen,
after almost ritually brandishing their fishhooks in the air, cast
their lines into the waves, usually catching something. Strong,
dark-skinned boys take off their open shirts and leap from the
seawall into the water in a show of foam, splashing about
while floating close to shore. Groups of people talk as they
stroll along the wide promenade by the ocean. The statue of
Jupiter at the top of the Business Exchange Building seems to
lean to greet La Giraldilla on another old Spanish fortress, El
Castillo de la Fuerza. The moon has indeed come out on the

other side of the ocean. Or is it just El Morro lighthouse that provides the glow? Whichever it is, the light pours down in torrents, shining also on the crowded ferryboats crossing the bay toward Regla or Casablanca. There seems to be the opening of an American film tonight at the Payret movie theater: the length of the line is overwhelming; from Paseo del Prado to San Rafael Street, people keep joining in, causing a commotion. You were watching it all, and in seventh heaven. I saw you sliding down the railing to the terrace below, where there was a sign saying NO TRESPASSING or something like that. I don't think I did try to stop you; besides, I'm sure you wouldn't have let me. Isn't that true? Answer me! Anyway, I called out to you, but you didn't even hear me. You leaned over into the void again. Instead of the dark, foul-smelling Hudson, the glittering sea rose up to a sky where there was no room for more stars to shine. Floating over the waves, entire palm groves were coming, fanning their fronds. Tall and proud, they came rumbling all along the West Side, which immediately disappeared, and was covered by the Paseo del Prado. Coconut palms, laurels, banana trees, taro plants, *almácigos,* and trumpetwoods came sailing by, almost obliterating the entire island of Manhattan and its majestic towers and lengthy tunnels. A row of *corozo* palms linked Riverside Drive to the beaches of Marianao. The stretch from Calle de Reina to Paseo de Carlos III was all covered with trumpetwoods. The *salvaderas,* Santa Maria trees, laurels, *jiquíes, curujeyes,* and hibiscus were overtaking Lexington Avenue all the way to Calzada de Jesús del Monte. The balconies of buildings on Monserrate Street seemed to disappear behind the coconut palm fronds, and nobody would ever imagine that this avenue, so green and tropical, could have ever been named Madison Avenue. All of

Obispo Street was already a garden. The waves cooled the roots of the almond trees, the *guásimas,* the tamarinds, the *jutabanes,* and other trees and shrubs, weary perhaps after their long journey. A ceiba tree appeared suddenly at Lincoln Center (which was still standing) and instantly turned it into Parque de la Fraternidad. A myrobalan tree curved its branches, and Parque del Cristo appeared beneath it. 23rd Street was overcome with *nacagüitas*—who would think that it had once been New York's 5th Avenue? Way downtown a banyan tree popped up, and it shaded La Rampa and the National Hotel. From Old Havana up to the East Side, which was already fading, from Arroyo Apolo to the World Trade Center, now converted into the Loma de Chaple; from Luyanó up to the beaches of Marianao, all of Havana was a huge arboretum, where streetlights swayed like giant fireflies. All along the lighted paths people are strolling, carefree, joining in small groups and then scattering, to partially reappear later under the foliage of some arbor. Others, reaching the coastline, let the ebb and flow of the waves bathe their feet. The rumors of the whole city, loaded with conversation and the rustle of trees, completely filled you, refreshed you. And you jumped. This time—I read it in your face—you felt sure you were going to make it, that you would succeed in merging again with your own people, in being yourself again. At that moment I couldn't possibly think otherwise. It couldn't—it shouldn't—be any other way. But the loud siren of that ambulance has nothing to do with the ocean waves; those people, down below, like a multicolor anthill, crowd around you, but they cannot identify you. I went down. For the first time you had made New York look at you. Traffic stopped all along 5th Avenue. Sirens, whistles, dozens of patrol cars. A real spectacle. There is nothing more compelling than a disaster; a body plummeting into the void is a magnet that no one can resist. It must be looked at, inspected. Don't think that it was easy to get you back. But nothing material is really hard to obtain in this world controlled by castrated, stupefied pigs. You need only to find the slot and drop in a quarter—did you hear me? I said "quarter" in perfect English! Just as Margaret Thatcher herself would have pronounced it, though I don't know if Thatcher ever needed to use that word. . . . Luckily I had some money (I've always been very careful with my money, as you know). And I pronounced "cremation," "last wishes," and things like that beautifully. All I had to do was to place you in your damned narrow niche—Did you notice? It almost sounded like a tongue twister—but why should I leave you in that cold, small, dark place, together with so many small-minded, spoiled, terrible people, together with all those decrepit old people? Who would care if some of the ashes were or were not put in a hole? Who would bother to find out about such nonsense? Besides, who really cared about you? I did. I always did. I was the only one. And I wasn't going to let them put you in that wall among surely horrendous people with names one can't pronounce. Once more I had to find the slot and fill the piggy bank's belly.

I don't know how it is looked on in New York for someone to walk out of a cemetery with a suitcase in hand. The fact is that I did and nobody seemed to mind. A taxi, a plane, a bus, and here we are, once again at the southernmost point in the U.S.A. After I took you for a ride all over Key West—notice how well I pronounce it now—I didn't want to part from you without taking you along on this ride; without my taking this ride with you. How many times I told you that this was the place, that there was a place that looks like, that is almost the same as, the one over there. Why didn't you listen to me? Why did you not want to come along with me each time I came? Maybe just to annoy me, or because you didn't want to be convinced, or maybe because you thought it was cowardly to accept a half solution, a kind of merciful but inevitable mutilation that would have allowed you, at least partly, to recover some of your senses, your sense of smell perhaps, or part of your eyesight. But your soul, your soul had surely remained over there, where it always had been (it will never be able to liberate itself), watching your shadow wander through noisy streets here and among people who prefer to have you touch anything but their car. *Don't touch my car! Don't touch my car!* But I'll touch it! Do you hear me? And besides I'll kick it, and I'll get a stick and smash the windows, and out of these events I'll write a story (I have it almost finished) to prove to you that I can still write; and I will learn to speak Aramaic and Japanese and medieval Yiddish if I need to, so as never to have to go back to a city that has a Malecón, an old Spanish fortress with a lighthouse, or an avenue flanked with marble lions, leading to the sea. Listen carefully: I am the one who has triumphed, because I have survived and I will survive. Because my hatred is greater than my nostalgia. Much greater, much greater. And it keeps on growing. I think that no one on this key is watching over me or actually gives a damn if I go close to the seashore with a suitcase. If I were over there, I would have been arrested already, do you hear me? With a suitcase and by the seashore, what else could I be doing but boarding a rowboat, or an illegal ship, or even floating away on an inner tube or a raft that would drag me away from hell. Away from the exact same hell where you're headed right now. Did you hear me? Where you—I'm convinced—want to go. Are you listening? . . . I am opening the suitcase. I'm taking the lid off the box where you are, a bit of gray ashes with a tinge of blue. I touch you for the last time. For the last time I want you to feel my hands, the way I'm sure you feel them, touching you. For the last time, what we are made of will join together, we'll mingle with each other. . . . Good-bye now. Go soaring, sailing away. Like that. Let yourself be carried away by the currents, let them propel you and take you all the way back. Sea of Sargasso, ominous ocean, divine waters, accept my treasure; don't reject my friend's ashes; in the same way that while over there, desperate and infuriated, both of us begged you so many times to bring us to this place, and you did. Take him now to the other shore and lay him down gently on the place he hated so much, where he was made to suffer so much, from which he managed to escape, and far away from which he could not go on living.

New York, July 1982